DUNGER

JOY COWLEY

DUNGER

GECKO PRESS

This edition first published in 2013 by Gecko Press
PO Box 9335, Marion Square, Wellington 6141, New Zealand
info@geckopress.com

Distributed in New Zealand by Random House NZ
Distributed in Australia by Scholastic Australia
Distributed in the United Kingdom by Bounce Sales & Marketing
Distributed in the United States by Lerner Publishing Group

A catalogue record for this book is available from the
National Library of New Zealand.

ARTS COUNCIL OF NEW ZEALAND TOI AOTEAROA

Gecko Press acknowledges the generous support of
Creative New Zealand

Cover by Keely O'Shannessy, New Zealand
Typesetting by Vida & Luke Kelly, New Zealand
Printed in China by Everbest Printing Co Ltd,
an accredited ISO 14001 & FSC certified printer
ISBN paperback: 978-1-877579-46-2

For more curiously good books, visit www.geckopress.com

For Vita and Tom, and their Mum and Mumma.
Thank you for the love you share with the world.
— *Joy*

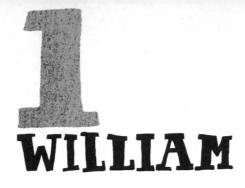

WILLIAM

The world is full of calamity: famines and wars, birds choking to death on oil spills, earthquakes, tsunamis, and Melissa – my disaster of a sister. Reading this, you'll probably say, what's wrong with this kid? Is he a bit paranoid? My response is that all tragedies are relative to their context and as far as domestic upheavals go, this one is about eight on the Richter scale.

Melissa might be fourteen – but fourteen what? The I.Q. of someone who thinks manga is some kind of tropical fruit? The number of times an hour she consults a mirror when she should be looking at www.hireabrain. com? Trust me, fourteen years is not an indication of her emotional or intellectual age.

The disaster all began with Melissa's baby-sitting job. She took the job not because she likes kids, but because she wanted money to buy clothes. So it was some karmic principle, like reap what you sow, that had her walking over the Wilsons' bouncy castle in shoes with heels like sharpened pencils.

Of course I call her an idiot. Who wouldn't?

"He's just jealous because I had a real job!" Melissa

shouts across the breakfast table, and she reminds our parents of an incident a whole year before, when I broke Dad's laptop (pure accident – I tripped over the cord).

I smile and exhale slowly, directing my breath over her yoghurt and muesli, which notches up her screeching by a decibel or two.

"You evil little monster!" Her hands cover the bowl. "Mum? Make him behave!"

Mum, or Mother-of-the-hundred-eyes as I like to call her, nudges me with her elbow. "Stop it, you two! I'm sick of you fighting like a couple of cats."

"Our insurance doesn't cover damage to other people's property," Dad says.

"The Wilsons must be insured," I remind him.

"Not for third-party damage." He has that weary old-man voice. "We'll find the money. Somehow."

At this point, you should know there is a fundamental flaw in my father. I'm not complaining, merely observing that while he may be a very good radiologist, a personality x-ray would show him completely lacking in survival instinct. He takes on all the family problems, regardless of whose they are, but does he try to solve them? No. He simply rolls over like a big dog, waves his paws in the air, and lets the world take advantage of him. Mum actually admires him for it. I don't. As far as I'm concerned, if my sister is old enough to wear stupid spiky shoes, she can accept responsibility for any damage they cause. I confess, however, to disappointment that I didn't witness the bouncy castle deflating on that little kid's birthday party. It must have been quite memorable.

Dad runs his forefinger slowly around the rim of his coffee cup; not a good sign. I have the feeling he is going to disregard all the practical advice I've offered, and I'm right. He breathes deeply and Mum reaches across the table to put her hand over his in a way that suggests she knows what he is going to say.

"We've decided," says Dad, "to work over the summer."

"Apart from the holiday in Queenstown," Melissa says quickly.

Mum looks at Dad and says, "We have to cancel the Queenstown trip."

My sister's spoon skids across the table and clatters on the floor. "No!"

"I'm afraid it's true." Dad is still trying to hypnotise his cup.

"But we have to go to Queenstown!" Melissa's eyes are as round as plums. "It's all been arranged! I told Herewini and Jacquie. They're going. And the McKenzies – the whole family! You can't do this!"

Dad doesn't answer. It's Mum who says, "We already have."

"What?" I'm appalled at the injustice. Last year Melissa went to Queenstown with a netball team. I've never been there. The week in January – luge, gondola, jet boating – was destined to be a major part of my education. Now I am the innocent victim of my sister's extraordinary stupidity.

I point this out to my father, who doesn't respond but instead – predictably – leaves my mother to do the talking.

She says, "I'm sorry, Will. We have to be practical."

I try to sound reasonable, logical even. "There is a point of family law here. You told us 'never break a promise', and if I remember correctly, the trip to Queenstown was actually a promise."

Melissa dives in. "Yes! You can't go back on a promise!"

"The promise still stands," says our mother, "it's just postponed for a year. Not this summer. I'm sure you'll both find plenty to do around here."

"Both?" I am determined to keep my voice level. "Please, Mother, do not include me in this fiasco. You may feel obliged to accept some parental responsibility since you allowed Melissa to buy shoes that turned out to be weapons of mass destruction. I, on the other hand, am blameless. I rest my case."

"Don't talk such rot, Will." She gets up and starts clearing the table. "This is not just about the bouncy castle. It's the recession. A lot of families have to cut back and frankly, for a number of reasons, we can't afford an expensive holiday. I know you and Melissa are disappointed, but by next year we'll have enough saved."

"You could get a bank loan!" Melissa cries. "Like you got to build the garage."

"That's different. A garage is an investment. Which one of you is going to empty the dishwasher?"

Our mother always does this; when argument fails

she pushes the escape button into domestic trivia, so of course Lissy and I know better than to respond.

I ask, "What precisely is the 'plenty' you expect us to do here when we should be in Queenstown?"

She turns the toaster upside down and shakes crumbs into the sink. "You could spend some time helping out at the shop."

Oh yes, indeed. A fine substitute for a helicopter flight to the top of the Tasman Glacier: Mum's book and stationery store, where it's my job to carry heavy boxes, sort magazines and newspapers, and clean up after kids who run riot because their mothers are talking to mine, while Melissa – oh yes, my sister. Where's she in this scenario? Out back in the toilet, reading romantic slush about vampires. No, thank you.

Dad sits back in his chair and folds his arms. "The rest of the time, you'll have a holiday with your grandparents. They want you to stay at the bach."

"You have got to be joking!" says Melissa.

My father never jokes about his parents, which probably explains a lot. I suppose the only way he survived growing up with those crazy people was to learn the fine art of submission. What I can't understand is why he would want to inflict them on us. An afternoon visit, two or three times a year, is surely more than enough.

"They want to go back to their old bach in the Sounds," Dad says. "They're too old to look after it on their own. You can be sure they'll give you a good time."

Oh, absolutely, sure. Like the day we spent at their

house in Timaru: a hilarious time playing cards and listening to them fight about who had forgotten to flush the toilet.

I shake my head slowly at my father, expressing disbelief that he could even suggest such a thing as a holiday with his parents.

Melissa gets up and bangs her chair against the table. "I'd rather die first!" she says, sweeping out of the room.

For the first time in my life, I find myself agreeing with my sister. Compared to a summer vacation with Grandma and Grandpa, death by slow torture would be a pleasure.

2

MELISSA

There's something a bit weird about my eleven-year-old brother. When he was nine he started talking like a dictionary, and for no reason. It was more or less an overnight change from normal kid-language to using words as missiles. He has to be right about everything. Maybe it's some kind of inferiority complex. My friends think he's a nutcase.

This holiday cancellation can't just be about the holes in the bouncy castle. That's just an excuse. Bet you anything, Mum and Dad decided to scrub Queenstown long before it happened. And anyway, I only did what anyone would do, running in to rescue a kid that was bawling its lungs out. How did I know the vinyl was so flimsy? When I try explaining this to Mum, she asks, "Why didn't you take off your shoes first?"

"Mum! If I was drowning, would you kick off your shoes before you dived in to get me?"

She thinks about it. "No."

"Mother means no, she wouldn't rescue you," says Will.

I give him a bored look. "Don't bite your tongue, little brother. You'll poison yourself."

"So says the queen of venom," he snaps back.

"That's enough!" Mum grabs some dishes off the table. "I'm glad you've decided not to go to your grandparents. They don't deserve your atrocious behaviour."

"Way to go, Ma," I say.

Dad comes back to life, reaching out to Mum who is already walking to the dishwasher. "They'll be disappointed, Alice. They especially asked, and without Lissy and Will they won't –"

"Negative!" says Will. "Subject closed."

But Dad really seems desperate for us to go. "I think you'd enjoy it," he says, holding out his hands like a beggar.

This is downright sneaky. Now, take my friend Jacquie's dad, for example. He lays down the law, tells Jacquie what to do, and when she doesn't do it, he gets mad. You can say no to a father who's a bully. It's a lot harder to say no to one who looks as though he's going to cry, even if you know he's being blatantly manipulative.

"They're too old to climb ladders," he says. "He's had a hip replacement. She's got osteoarthritis and macular degeneration. She can't see well. They've both got mobility issues…"

"Dad, I'm not going." Will throws his spoon into his empty bowl and takes it over to Mum. "That is my final and ultimate answer."

"Me, too," I add.

Dad wipes his unshaven chin with his hand. It sounds gritty. "I must say it's not like you two, turning down good money."

"Money? What money?"

"I guess I haven't told you about that bit." He looks at Mum, then back at us. "They want to pay you. It's four years since they've been to the bach. They want a holiday, but can't manage on their own. They need help to clean up the place, get firewood, that sort of thing."

"How much money?" Will asks.

"Too much," Mum says quickly. "Far too much!"

I've already decided no amount of pocket money is going to make me go to a run-down bach with no electricity and those two, deaf as posts, shouting at each other, their weird clothes covered with food stains, and Grandpa's terrible driving in that old car with the window down so he can call other drivers rude names.

"How much?" insists Will.

Dad scratches his chin again. "Ten days at a hundred dollars a day." Then he says, "Each."

"I told you it's a ridiculous amount." Mum looks annoyed.

I am gobsmacked. It has to be a trick. One thousand dollars? Each? Not likely. If they have that kind of money to spare, why won't they give it to Dad so we can all go to Queenstown like we planned? There has to be a catch somewhere. I mean, those two old hippies look like homeless people and they're always going grumpo about the price of stuff. A thousand dollars each? To begin with, it wouldn't even be fair because I'm the oldest – it should be more like fifteen hundred for me and five hundred for Will. But I don't know.

Maybe they have got the dosh. Grandma's favourite quote is, "Say less than you know. Have more than you show." Although what about their car, that rusty old heap of junk? They can't even afford to get it painted. Is that not-showing, or proof they don't have a cent? Nah, the whole thing has to be some kind of scam.

"I'm not happy about the money," Mum says. "It wasn't my idea. Children should be willing to work for their grandparents for nothing. For love."

"They actually offered one thousand dollars each?" says Will.

"That's what they said." Dad smiles, sensing weakness. "You'll be expected to work for your wages."

I don't say anything because I still don't believe the money bit. One thousand dollars is about as real as bananas growing at the bottom of the sea. I mean, in the old days Grandma and Grandpa lived in a hippy commune, in something called a geodesic dome – a kind of igloo made of metal and plastic – and they made their own clothes, even sandals out of kelp seaweed, according to Dad. They got a bit respectable after that, and both became teachers, but I'll eat mud if they've ever had two thousand dollars to give away.

Will looks at me. I can practically see the dollar signs in his eyes. "I decline to call it wages," he says. "Let's think of it as compensation."

3

WILLIAM

If I explain the system of child slave labour that operates in my mother's bookshop, you might understand why my rigid policy regarding grandparents suddenly has become flexible. I get a microscopic four dollars an hour for unpacking books and returning the out-of-date magazines. Actually, we don't return the entire magazine, just the cover, hence my job of tearing off covers to send back and putting the rest in the recycling.

Normally I'd describe my mother as a woman of good nature, but that aspect of her personality disappears where money is concerned. When I told her she was paying me less than one-third of the basic wage, she said I was an eleven-year-old getting perfectly good pocket money. I then pointed out that parents are obliged to give their children pocket money, regardless, to which she merely said, "Hard cheese!" Logic is not her strong point.

Ten days with my grandparents will not be a holiday but a prison sentence. I am prepared for that, and thanks to the predictable rotation of the earth, when ten days have passed, I'll have a brand new iPad.

Melissa still insists there is no money. When Dad assured her payment would be made, she said it was just a bribe but that she would go anyway, because it was the right thing to do. As if anyone would believe that. I'll bet she's already made a long shopping list of new clothes and shoes.

I've considered the outcome at great length, and definitely, yes, an iPad is a good investment, although if I shop wisely and get last year's model, I might also manage a second-hand skateboard. I should tell you here and now, I've never had either.

An iPad is essential for my education. With my own money, I can control my destiny. The future looks good. However, prison must come first.

As a condemned man, I made sure to eat a hearty breakfast of strawberry waffles and cream this morning, and I've packed enough milkshake lollies and biscuits to last the full sentence. I admit to a grave suspicion of food cooked without electricity by an almost-blind jailer.

Only a few hours ago, there we were at the bookshop – working, of course – with our bags in the storeroom out the back, waiting for our grandparents to arrive from Timaru. I was going through the magazines, my usual job, while Melissa showed a customer how to use the photocopier. Mum had put an orange traffic cone in the parking space outside the shop door, to save it for Grandpa's rust bucket. He's had the same car, a Vauxhall Velox, for an eternity and perhaps even longer.

I was wearing my usual Saturday gear. Melissa had

painted her face to look sixteen instead of fourteen and was wearing one of those outfits that has a top and a bottom and nothing in-between, so boys will look at her. She never has to tear covers off old magazines. Mum lets her work behind the counter, which she loves because she can do her pouty lipstick smiles for the boys when Mum's not looking. It doesn't work for my mates, though. When they come in, she just gives them the dead-fish look.

The shop is long and narrow, and I was at the back putting bar code labels on writing pads when the Vauxhall ran over the traffic cone. I missed the fuss. First thing I knew, Mum was taking the label machine out of my hand and saying, "They're here, Will. You'd better get your bag."

It's actually her bag I've borrowed, the one with wheels, and as I got it out of the storeroom, I heard my grandparents. They are deaf, but too stubborn to get hearing aids, so they're always shouting at each other.

"Silly old fool!" Grandma yelled. "I told him to stop. 'You're going to hit it,' I said. He never listens!"

The day was warm but she was wearing a thick lumpy jumper and earrings made of peacock feathers. Her hand wobbled on the handle of her walking stick but there was no way of knowing if that was a permanent shake or just because she was angry with Grandpa.

"Oh, shut up!" he yelled back.

His clothes looked normal except that his jacket sleeves ended way above his wrists. Since he hasn't grown lately, I assume it was someone else's hand-me-down jacket, probably from an op shop. He shouted at Mum, "No shilly-shallying, Alice. Let's get them in the carriage and whip the horses. There's a long ride ahead."

"I told him to stop!" Grandma said. "He deliberately did it!"

"Don't worry about the cone," Mum said. "It's not important."

Lissy gave me a nervous look as we wheeled our bags into the shop. I stepped forward. "Good morning, Grandma. Good morning Grandpa."

They smiled but didn't move. Grandma scanned us and her gaze rested on Melissa. "Cover yourself up, girl!" she bellowed. "You'll get a death of cold in your kidneys!"

Lissy flushed red. She opened her mouth to argue, then her lips went small and round like a raspberry doughnut, and slowly made something resembling a smile. That's how I knew my sister finally believed the money was real.

MELISSA

When Grandma made me put on a T-shirt, my little-creep brother smiled from ear to ear. I was furious. I know all about the 1960s. I've seen the film *Hair*. People in communes grew more than vegetables in their organic gardens and they didn't care if they walked around naked – so what's the problem with a bare stomach? Kidneys, my foot! As for the smirking brother, his grin disappeared when he found out he had to sit in the front of the car with Grandpa, reading the map and yelling directions into a hairy deaf ear. William might sound as though he knows everything but he's useless at map-reading. Served him right when he mixed up left and right, and got shouted at for directing Grandpa into Christchurch airport instead of the road north out of town.

So now Grandma's in the back with me, but she fell asleep almost as soon as we left the shop and since she's as deaf as Grandpa, his shouting doesn't wake her up. When the old man gets mad, his comments get a bit disconnected from reality, like when we found ourselves on the road to the airport and he bellowed, "I didn't come here for a haircut!" And then, when we had to stop at a red light and the car in front was a bit slow in moving on green, he yelled out the window, "What colour are you waiting for? Purple?"

Grandma sleeps through it all, making a breathing noise, not quite a snore, that flutters her peacock-feather earrings. Her hair is bright orange with two centimetres of grey at the scalp, and with her pillow she takes up three-quarters of the seat, which is okay because I don't need much space, just a corner to sit and text Jacquie and Herewini and tell them I'm about to make my fortune. I make sure to mention the amount for two reasons: first, so they'll stop being sorry for me having parents too poor to take me to Queenstown; and second, so they'll eat their hearts out with envy. A thousand bucks is a lot of money. But they're my best friends so I might buy them a little something afterwards like a scarf or a belt.

If I can't be with my friends, at least we can text each day. When I packed my cell phone charger, the brother-creep laughed at me. "They don't have electricity!" he said, which I already knew. But I'm sure I can easily introduce myself to Grandma's neighbours or a shop that won't mind if I plug it in. Dad says the old bach is the only house without power. Nice neighbours. Problem solved.

Grandma wakes up with a snort at Kaikoura when Grandpa brakes to avoid hitting a truck full of sheep. She swears at him, then tells him it's time for lunch so he should pull in at a teashop.

"Time for the F word," Grandpa says cheerfully. He always says it. He means Food and he thinks it's funny. Actually, he thinks all his jokes are hilarious.

Will turns his head. "It's called a café, Grandma. They serve cups of tea in *cafés*."

"So be it, Einstein," she says. "You find us one."

Occasionally, Will can be practical. In seconds, he spots a place close to a free car park, and I'm helping Grandma get her swollen ankles out of the car, feet on ground, walking stick in hand. She doesn't say thanks, but that's okay, it's my job. She's awfully slow, she and Grandpa both, and they sit at the table nearest the door, puffing after the five steps up from the street.

Grandpa waves some money at us. "A pot of tea and sandwiches for us, and get what you like for yourselves."

Will and I are looking along the glass case at sandwiches and custard tarts when I spot this awesome bit of eye-candy behind the counter. He's so very cool, with long floppy hair and eyes like wet bath mats. He reminds me a bit of Mr Leverton, our geography teacher. I think it's really pathetic the way my friends carry on about Mr Leverton. He might have a Hollywood smile, but as far as I'm concerned, it's a waste of time being a fan. He's too old, he's a teacher, and he's engaged.

"Can I help you?" the café guy says.

I flash back a smile. "Yes, please."

I'm wearing my yellow outfit, a halter top with just a bit of padding in the bra, and a short skirt that sits neatly on my hips, but you know what? It's all buried under the extremely hideous T-shirt Grandma made me wear. Fortunately, it doesn't matter because the guy sees me – you know, really *looks* at me, as though I'm the only person in the room. He doesn't even talk to Will. When he gives me the change, he touches the palm of my hand, making a shiver go down my back. "I'll bring the tea and milkshakes over," he says.

He does, too. He comes out from the counter, absolutely drop-dead gorgeous, holding a tray in one hand like a professional waiter. As he leans over my chair to put the tray on the table, he sort of accidentally on purpose puts his other hand on my back and leaves it there.

Grandma grabs the teapot and says, "You know she's only thirteen."

The hand goes away.

I am furious with Grandma, "I'm not thirteen!"

"She's fourteen years, seven months and nine days," says Will.

I turn to look at Mr Gorgeous but his face is like a window with the blind drawn down. He smiles politely at Grandma and Grandpa and says, "Enjoy your lunch."

Back in the car, Grandma tells me how forgetful she is; how once, when unpacking the grocery order, she put the toilet rolls in the freezer and a packet of frozen chicken wings in the bathroom cupboard. I think she expects me to laugh, but I don't. I look out the window. You can't tell me she didn't know the age of her only granddaughter. But if she thinks I'm worried about it, she's got another think coming. I couldn't care less. I mean, he's not the only hot guy on the planet.

After her long sleep and lunch, Grandma's very chatty, but it's all about her, on and on. Not once does she ask me about my position in the netball A team, not even a question about school and the subjects I'll be taking next year. What I get is her varicose veins and what the eye specialist said about her sight and how she used to go fishing at the bach for huge snapper. She doesn't even talk about Dad, her own son. She is extremely self-absorbed.

5

WILLIAM

I admit to curiosity concerning the famous bach. Dad always talks about childhood holidays there as "twelve on a scale of one to ten". Lissy and I have never been there. I remember there were invitations, but Mum always said she couldn't take children to a place with no electricity and an outdoor toilet. So why is she sending us there now, on our own? You have no doubt discovered, as I have, that parents can practise grand deceit, yet look extremely injured when their child tells a tiny white lie. Such is the pecking order in families. Mind you, I'm not complaining, just saying that the bach could be interesting. Unlike Melissa who only packed a cell phone charger, I have a torch with spare batteries, a compass, my Swiss Army knife, and the survival rations already mentioned.

"The chimney will be brimming with birds' nests," Grandpa says cheerfully. "That'll be your first job. Clean it out, so's we can light the fire."

"I thought my first job was map-reading." I don't say it all that loud but his ear scoops it up.

"Map ain't no job." He puts on his cowboy accent.

"You gotta do better than that, pardner. Lasso the ladder! Break in the chimney!"

I keep my finger on the map because we're approaching Havelock. "I think we turn right to get on the Sounds road."

"Chuck that thing away, pardner. From here on in, I know the way like I know my own ask-your-mother-for-sixpence. Me and the horse can go there blindfold."

Grandma leans over and pokes me in the back. "Don't take any notice of the old fool. You hang on to that map, Will, or he'll have us up a tree. We've got to get there well before dark."

"Why?" Melissa sounds nervous, probably thinking of werewolves and vampires or the fact that she packed a cell phone charger instead of a torch.

"I don't see too well," Grandma says.

Grandpa turns off on the Sounds road, and I get our first view of water and green hills. Dad has told us tales of a narrow dirt road, winding into wilderness like a never-ending snake, but I think that was pure hyperbole. The road is curvy but sealed and there are houses everywhere, almost suburban.

The old folk get excited when they recognise familiar landmarks, the bay where there was a bush fire back in 1972 and the house with the jetty that once belonged to a circus lion tamer. It amuses me that Grandpa can remember all this trivia and yet forget my name. Twice, he has called me Alistair – my father's name – and for the rest of the time it's some substitute like boyo or pardner or tama, depending on which accent he's trying out.

"Are we nearly there?" Melissa asks.

"About two hours, girlie," says Grandpa.

"Two hours!"

"One and a half," Grandma says.

"It's two hours from here, you daft old chook," Grandpa shouts. "You've forgotten!"

"You want a bet? One hour, thirty minutes!"

"Two! You'd forget your head if it wasn't screwed on, and mark my words, you'd be better off without it. Two hours!"

They've started one of their stupid arguments, and it goes on for about five kilometres until it's time for a toilet stop. Only there aren't any toilets, just bushes at the side of the road. Melissa is full of Dad's stories about possums and wild pigs, and she refuses to get out of the car. But she is also full of milkshake and bottles of water, so she has to get out after we've all finished. She still won't go into the trees, so she squats down on the road behind the car where we can't see her. Too bad another car comes along.

Silly Lissy! She never gets it right. She jumps into the back seat, screaming at us all for laughing, and then she opens her cell phone to text her friends and shut us out. Bet she's not texting what just happened, though.

I have to admit that Dad is right about the road. It gets much narrower and there are fewer houses, an occasional farm but mainly forest with tree ferns and manuka hanging over the edges of the dirt road in front of us. Sometimes, we glimpse the sea through a clearing. Grandpa tells me that the black lines in a bay are a mussel farm, but I don't see any boats. I get a feeling we're going nowhere. Well, the nearest thing to nowhere.

The sun shines low on the water and the trees cast long shadows on the road. If I were a poet I could write something about sunset in the Sounds, but I'm William, eleven and a half years old and just plain worried. Do they really expect me to clean a chimney in the dark?

I check my watch. One hour and forty minutes since the argument. We have now taken another turn-off and are on a track that isn't a road. Grass grows down the middle and ferns brush the car on each side. The ruts reveal how primitive the springs are in these old cars. Whoa! If I didn't have a seat belt on, I'd flatten my face on the windscreen.

The track takes us down to the edge of a bay that is half in sunlight and half in dark shadow. On the shadowed side there's a stand of old macrocarpa trees. Grandpa pulls over and stops. Neither he nor Grandma says a word.

"Are we here?" I ask.

I already know it. Inside the circle of trees is a wooden hut with a brick chimney, a verandah, a water tank and a corrugated iron garage. The grass and scrub around them have grown almost as high as the hut's windows.

This is the famous bach of my father's childhood.

6
MELISSA

There are no neighbours, the nearest town is Havelock and my phone battery is flat. I can't stand it. I really can't. But I don't know what to do.

Grandma says, "If you get desperate, you can use our phone. Mind you, it's a party line shared by three houses."

There is hope. "How far away are they?"

"The nearest is the Hoffmeyers but they're going to the North Island during the week. Then there's Emily Adamson – no, she died and I heard her house was for sale. Maybe our phone won't be busy. But right now, you'd better get busy, my girl. The car has to be unpacked before dark."

That's my job, wading through the long grass to the car and back to the cottage with boxes of food and clothes, the wet weeds around my legs full of creepy things I can't see. Dad talked about wasps in the Sounds. Suppose I tread on a wasps' nest? Those things can kill you.

"Put the boxes on the table!"

The inside of the bach isn't too bad, except it stinks. There's a wooden table with a pile of flax tablemats at one end, and a big pottery bowl where I'm supposed to put the fruit. The floor is made of bare boards that creak a bit, and the rugs look handmade. I guess that the blankets on the couch, patchwork and crochet, are also handmade, which sort of goes along with Dad's stories about the hippy era. Grandma lights candles and stands them along the table and bench. "Tomorrow I'll get the lanterns sorted," she says, pointing to a couple of old-fashioned lanterns, the kind you see in movies, hanging from the ceiling. "Take a candle to help you see in the cupboards."

When I open the first kitchen cupboard, I nearly drop the candle. The shelves are covered with mouse poo. I can't put food in there!

"What's wrong, girl?"

"Mice, Grandma. They're everywhere, thousands of droppings!" I shudder and so does the candle flame. "They smell bad!"

"Clean it, then," she says.

I hold my breath as I take out all the cans and boxes in the cupboard – old, out-of-date food that has to be thrown away – then I get a hearth brush and sweep out the shelves. When I've finished, the cupboard still pongs like a mouse toilet. I'll have to scrub it clean. Grandma gives me a bucket and I turn on the kitchen tap. It rattles but nothing comes out.

"Well now, that's another job for the morning," says Grandma. "Just leave the boxes of food on the table. Somewhere in the car there's drinking water, so we won't shrivel up in the night."

"What about a shower?"

"Eh?"

"I really need a shower!"

"Have a swim," she says, "but watch out for the sharks."

I finish unpacking the car. Grandpa has opened the garage door and the ladder is now up against the side of the house. Will is up there, banging around on the iron roof and poking the handle of a rake down the chimney. It's quite dark now. He could miss his footing. With one day over and nine to go, it would be a real pain if he gets a broken leg. "You be careful!" I yell.

Grandpa comes into the kitchen to look at the black wood-stove. He opens a little door at the base of the chimney and straw pokes out. "Just as I thought, chock-a-block," he says. "No way but to burn it out."

He calls Will down the ladder, and gives him a kerosene-soaked rag and a box of matches. I stand below, with Grandma leaning on her stick, and we watch as Will climbs back up the ladder, pushes the rag down the chimney and drops a lit match. I expect an explosion, but it's just yellow flame, some sparks against the dark sky, and a crackling inside the bricks. In about five minutes the birds' nests have fallen down as ash in the stove, and Grandpa is saying, "Most effective, boyo," which has my brother acting like he's just invented a cure for cancer.

Grandpa sets some paper and pine cones in the fire part of the stove. "Time for the F word. Chicken with potatoes and gravy. How does that sound?" He strikes a match, then says, "Oh dammit!" and blows it out. "We can't!" He looks at me and Will. "This stove heats the water and since there's no water, a fire will bust the pipes."

"Another thing for the morning," Grandma says.

The candlelit dinner is cold baked beans with bread, but that doesn't matter because I'm too tired to eat.

Grandma gives us sheets to make up the bunks in the spare room. "Will takes the top bunk. Melissa, you're on the bottom."

But Will refuses to sleep in the same room as me, and in a childish tantrum, he takes his sheets out to the couch in the living room.

I borrow a word from Grandpa. "Good-oh."

7

WILLIAM

The birds wake me up. There must be millions of them, all chirping at once. I open the back door and smell a mix of wet grass and sea, better than the mouse-poo stink that fills the house. I had this idea that the long-drop toilet would be the stinkiest place, but it isn't, probably because it hasn't been used for four years. It is full of cobwebs, some of them across the hole. I think my pee might break them, but the webs just sag like old curtains, and I don't drown any spiders. The hole under the cobwebs is very deep. All I can see at the bottom is some old yellow newspaper, now wet.

When I come out, there's blue smoke by the garage. Grandpa is up. He's made a fire with wood in half a drum with a bit of reinforcing iron over the top to hold a pot of water. I look up at the chimney, remembering the mission so well accomplished last night.

Grandpa is already dressed. "Want a cup of coffee?"

"I'd rather have cocoa, if that's all right."

He pours hot water into two mugs. It's coffee but it's made with condensed milk and tastes all right. I sit beside him on a log and look around at the place in morning light. Growing around the bach are eight macrocarpa trees, big, with lumpy trunks and sprawling branches, and beyond the car I can see some of the bay, the water a dark green colour with glints of light. In the other direction, behind the bach, there is a hill covered with native bush, mostly manuka, I think. I ask, "Is that where the water comes from?"

"What's that?"

"The water." I point. "Is the stream up there?"

"Yep."

I say to him, "I fixed the chimney. Maybe I can solve the water problem, too."

He doesn't answer, but just sits staring at the hill and slurping his coffee. I wonder if he has ever thought about getting a hearing aid. He takes his time. When he has sucked the last drop from his mug, he stands, rubbing his knees. "Put your gumboots on," he says. "We'd better see to the water."

Going up the hill is hard work, even for me. The path is overgrown with scrub that gets thicker, and Grandpa has to stop every few steps to get his breath. We come to a place where we can't go on – the bush is far too dense. I turn and look back. The sun is still behind the hill and the bay is green, dark in the shadows. Everything smells wet, as though the tide has come over it during the night. Grandpa points sideways with his stick and says, "Better go up the stream." For once he's not shouting. It's more of a gaspy whisper. But at least he knows where the stream is, not far to our left, through some trees and down a bit of a bank. He digs his stick into the dry earth and leans on it, then he waves his free hand at me.

"Come on, you silly beggar!"

I realise he wants me to hold his hand and guide him down the slope, and I wonder how difficult it would be for him to say please. But I do it, and somehow get him to the water. It's not a big stream, about half a metre across, clear water running over stones with some tufts of moss and ferns at the edges. Near the edge, as far as I can see in either direction, is a black pipe, presumably the one that feeds water to the tank by the house.

I keep hold of Grandpa as we walk uphill through the water. It is shallow but the stones are slippery. Sometimes he grabs me so hard that I nearly fall over. Just as I think this is going to take the entire day, we see the end of the pipe up ahead. It is high and dry. The plastic bottle tied on the end is pointing downhill.

"It must have been a wild pig!" I shout. "It's pulled the pipe out of the stream."

"Nope. Rain." He holds his side and coughs the words. "Flood washes. Pipe out. Always." He takes a few breaths. "Always happens."

I pick up the end of the pipe. The bottle looks like a big detergent container and it has holes punched in it. I suppose that's for a filter. There's brown sediment in the bottom of the plastic.

Grandpa sits on the bank giving instructions while I take the bottle off the pipe and wash it. Then I have to pick up the pipe and whack it against the stones to dislodge any sediment that might have got through.

"If there's a blockage, it's up the top end," he says.

By now the sun is shining in bright patches through the bush and I'm starving. My arms are tired, scratched red with branches. I tie the bottle back on the hose end of the pipe, and Grandpa shows me where to scrape stones away so that the bottle is lying in a deep pool. He is very particular. I have to find larger stones to place on either side, then a big flat stone as a bridge to prevent the bottle from washing out.

When I've finished, he puts his hand on my shoulder. I think he's going to say something but he is just steadying himself in preparation for the climb back up the bank.

It takes just as long to get down the hill. I'm sure half the day has gone but it's only nine o'clock. Grandpa takes me to a tap on a post by the garage.

"This is the lowest outlet," he says, turning it on.

No water comes out. Not a drop! All that effort for nothing!

"Listen, boyo."

I hear a noise like a gurgling stomach.

Grandpa grins. "We're clearing the air lock. Wait!"

More gurgling noise and then comes a spurt of brown water.

Another spurt! Another! It gushes out of the pipe like a pulse, as though it is part of the hill's great artery system, and then, finally, it steadies as a clear flow.

Grandpa turns the tap off. "Anything happening to the tank?"

I listen. There is a sound like water dropping into a bucket. "It's filling!"

"Good-oh," says Grandpa. "I smell breakfast."

Grandma has been cooking pancakes in a frying pan on the outdoor fire. She has smothered them with sugar, butter and lemon juice, and there is a stack waiting for Grandpa and me, on the table.

"We've had ours. They're delicious," says Lissy. Then she sees my arms. "You've scratched yourself."

I shrug, my mouth full of food.

"You should have worn long sleeves," she says.

She sounds like Mother-of-the-hundred-eyes. "It's nothing," I tell her.

The water is running into the tank and the pipes to the house are now alive with it. Lissy turns on the tap at the sink and after a few spouts of brown, she gets clean water. I want to tell her, "You can thank me for that, Sis. I'm a first-class plumber."

She comes to the end of the table and looks at one of the boxes of food. "Grandma? Hey, Grandma? This bag of flour hasn't been opened."

Grandma is washing her spectacles under the tap and doesn't hear her.

"Grandma, what flour did you use?"

Carefully, Grandma wipes her glasses on a tea towel. "You don't waste good flour."

"Did you make pancakes with the flour out of the

cupboard?" Melissa screams. "It had mouse poo in it!"

Grandma puts her glasses back on. "I put it through the sifter," she says.

Melissa is hysterical, and I don't blame her. Even Grandpa stops eating. He says, "That might have sifted out the hard stuff, but what about the pee?" He pushes his plate away. "Mice carry bubonic plague, I'll have you know."

"You're wrong," Grandma shouts. "Bubonic plague is rats!"

I've had two pancakes and I feel sick. Very sick. Lissy is sitting on the couch, crying. "I want to go home!" she wails.

I rummage in my suitcase and get out a handful of milkshake lollies.

"What's that?" Lissy asks.

"Antibiotics," I tell her, and I drop some in her lap.

8
MELISSA

That is the worst thing that has ever happened to me, so extremely horrible that there are no words in the world to describe my feelings, and it's not over yet, I mean I could become ill with some fatal disease and I can't even use my phone. How could she do that? Make pancakes from flour poisoned by mice! I'll never forgive her as long as I live, and that might not be very long. Will ate only two pancakes. I had five.

They had a huge fight about it, Grandpa and Grandma, calling each other names like dimwit and bonehead. Eventually, Grandpa helps her take the old food outside, and Will digs a hole for it behind the garage. After that, Will and I have the job of taking everything out of containers and tipping it down the hole – flour, sugar, split peas, rice, baking powder, sundried tomatoes, golden syrup. Heaps of stuff, all stinking of mice.

"Why don't they just put it out in the rubbish?" I ask Will.

"No rubbish collection," he says.

"What do you mean, no rubbish collection?"

"Stupid question, Melissa. It's not city living, haven't you noticed? They have to recycle things. Organic stuff gets buried. Containers get washed and used again. Paper starts the fire. Cans and plastic are washed and stored in a sack for the next excursion to the Havelock dump."

"That is so primitive!" I shake out a bottle of tomato sauce, two years past its use-by date. It plops into the hole on top of some old tins of something unnamed and disturbs a small cloud of bluebottle flies. "This isn't a holiday, Will. We're living in some kind of useless TV survival programme."

"I got the water running again," he says. "That's useful."

"You helped Grandpa fix the water."

"No. He didn't do anything. I did it."

"Liar!"

"I did it all myself, Melissa, just ask him. So what were you doing while I was working up the hill? Painting your eyebrows? You knew Grandma couldn't see diddly-squat. You could at least have checked the flour before she cooked it."

The mere mention of flour goes directly to my stomach and sends a cold shiver through me. I refuse to argue with my brother and I walk inside to scrub the pantry shelves.

It's hot in the kitchen. Grandpa has the fire going in the stove and the water is already warm. I fill the bucket, add detergent and pine disinfectant, then look under the sink for rubber gloves. Of course, there aren't any. My nails will be ruined. But I do find a scrubbing brush, wooden with stiff bristles, and I scrub like heck all over the shelves and the sides and the doors of the cupboards. Mouse poo is tucked like seeds in the corners and I get every bit out and yes, my purple damson nail polish does get chipped, my hands get pink, and I have to change the water twice because it is so filthy. Scrub with brush. Wipe with cloth. Scrub, wipe, scrub, wipe. In the end those cupboards are extremely clean, even smelling clean. I empty the bucket and dry my hands that are so red, I'm not kidding, they look like they've been in a house fire.

Grandma gives me a tube of cream. "Rub that on, Melissa. Good job. Now we can put the groceries away."

I personally wash the plastic flour-container twice and sniff. No smell. But just to be sure I wash it a third time, drying it with a clean towel. I open the new bag of flour and pour it in, pure white, rising in a fine cloud as it flows.

Grandma says, "Oven's hot. Want to make some scones?"

I shake my head.

"Why not?" She laughs. "Good flour."

"I don't know how to make scones."

"What'd you say?"

"I've never made scones!" I mumble.

"Nothing to it, girl," she says. "Get the mixing bowl off that shelf, and I'll show you."

Actually, it's not all that difficult, flour with baking powder, some sugar, a pinch of salt, and rub in the butter. She tells me to squish the butter between my fingers so it mixes right into the flour and when that's done, I pour in milk to make a stiff dough. She puts a board on the table. "It's clean," she says, but I don't trust her eyes and wipe it again before turning out the dough.

"Flatten it thin," she tells me. "Put these chopped dates on it, fold it over and Bob's your uncle. That's right, you've got it. Now put it on the oven tray and cut it through, right through, into squares."

"How do I know if the oven's the right temperature?"

"You know by feel." She opens the oven door. "Yep, it's right. Slide the tray in. Not there. In the middle of the oven! Now close the door and wait."

"How long?"

"Until they smell cooked," she says.

I sit on the couch and reach for my phone. No good, I remember. Battery flat. So I look around the living room. It's very woody, with knotholes in the walls and ceilings; old black and white posters fastened to the walls with drawing pins. The pictures are real antiques, I'd say: photos of people I've never heard of – Bob Dylan; Joan Baez; Peter, Paul and Mary – everyone with funny haircuts and clothes, guitars without electrics, and the kind of microphones that look like ice cream in a cone. Dad said his father used to play the guitar. I can't imagine that, although I guess everyone was young once. I can't see myself growing old. If that happens I'll be like Mum's mother, Granny Margaret, with neat grey hair, a purry voice and smart dresses. My kitchen will be spotless and I'll have a Royal Albert tea set with roses to serve my grandchildren, not heavy pottery mugs that still look like the clay that made them. Except I won't have grandchildren because I probably won't have children, because there might not be time for that in a career of fashion design and travel to those famous *haute couture* shows. I mean, you have to work extremely hard to become somebody in the world of high fashion. The sophisticated lifestyle doesn't leave much space for things like bookshops and babies and taking x-rays of somebody's lungs. I've studied the magazines and I know that getting to the top in the fashion industry is very hard work.

"Scones cooked!" Grandma waves a towel in my face. "I said, your scones are done!"

Scones and kitchen cupboards are not the kind of hard work I have in mind.

9
WILLIAM

Lunch is buttered date scones, lemon cordial and a banana, all good. But I know for certain that Melissa's culinary skills extend to either cheese on toast or baked beans on toast, so she can't tell me she made these scones without step-by-step instructions from Grandma. As a joke, I ask, "What flour did you use?"

True Melissa-style, she tries to punch me, but I duck and she connects with my glass of lemonade. That also misses me and slops over Grandpa. Grandpa pushes his chair back. There's lemonade on the table and down the front of his shirt and shorts. He says to me, "You clean it up, laddie."

"I didn't do it! She did!"

"You started it, so you finish it," he growls.

When there's a thousand dollars at stake, it doesn't pay to argue. Although I am furious, I get the dishcloth from the sink and wipe the table. I throw the cloth back on the bench. Somehow I always get the fallout from Melissa's stuff-ups. I refuse to return to my chair and instead sit on the end of the couch near the bookcase.

After a bit of silence, Grandpa bellows, "Some books

over there you might like to read, *Swiss Family Robinson, Man in the Iron Mask...*"

I shout back, "I read those when I was six." In fact, I was eight, but in these circumstances, I feel I have a right to a margin of deliberate error.

So then it's Grandma who yells, "What kind of books do you like?"

"Science fiction," I tell her.

"Ray Bradbury!" says Grandma. She turns to Grandpa. "Honey, give him that book, you know – Ray Bradbury."

"I know all about him," I tell her. "Dad's got Ray Bradbury. He's ancient."

Grandpa holds the edge of the table and levers himself out of his chair. "Will and I have a lot to do," he says. "We've only cracked the ice on the garage clean-up."

There's a sudden noise in the kitchen, three beeps sounding like a microwave, except there is no microwave, so it must be an alarm of some sort. As Grandpa pushes his chair away, the beeps happen again and I realise it's the phone, an ancient black thing sitting on a green shelf by the cupboards. It's so old, it doesn't even have a dial, just a handle at the side.

"Three shorts," says Grandma. "That's our number – 308S."

Grandpa picks up the phone and bellows, "You there? Hullo? Oh, it's you." He turns to Grandma. "The A-Team."

The A-Team is what they call Mum and Dad, Alice and Alistair. Grandma leans on her stick to get out of her chair, and hobbles over, grabbing impatiently at Grandpa's arm. They swap the phone between them, back and forth, shouting things like, "They're fine!" "Everything's hunky-dory!"

When Grandma says, "We're getting on like a house on fire," Melissa says to me, "Yeah, we're burned out," and although I am not feeling funny, I can't help but laugh.

They talk for ages, then it's our turn. Mum's voice seems very far away, reminding me of the galactic distance between us and them. But there is not much I can say with the old couple standing nearby, so both Melissa and I have this case of severe verbal constipation, absolutely bursting yet unable to let out more than a little puff of a word here, a word there. "Yeah, good." "Okay." "Yes." "No." "It's all right."

Neither of us mentions mice.

Instead of making us feel better, the phone call has sent us spiralling down into homesickness. We've been away just over twenty-four hours but it seems like forever.

I go out to the garage with Grandpa to continue the clean-up, sorting through boxes of rusted bolts, screws, hinges, and tins of old hardened paint. When I find two tins of green roof paint, he prises open the lids with a screwdriver and says it's still fine, good enough to paint the garage. I don't comment but I guess that will be my next job.

We haven't been out there very long before Grandma comes out with Melissa. "Tide's in," Grandma says.

Grandpa straightens up and feels his back. "Okey-dokey, shall we go and pay our respects to Tangaroa?"

I'm not sure how to answer. At school we learned that Tangaroa is the god of the sea, but Grandpa has Irish ancestry.

"He means go for a swim," Grandma says.

I still don't know what to say, because last night I heard Grandma tell Lissy to watch out for sharks, and there's no way I'm getting into water that has Jaws swimming around looking for a feed. But I confess to a small curiosity. Half the day has passed and we haven't yet been to the beach.

So that's what we do, walk down the drive, across the narrow gravel road, through some long grass to a short strip of flat stones above flat water. There are no waves. The sea is so calm, it barely moves. Further out, a bird dives straight down and splashes. "That there's a gannet," says Grandpa.

The way he says it, makes me answer, "I know."

We've already told them we don't want to swim, but they keep insisting that we'll enjoy it. Grandpa tells me, "When I was your age they couldn't get me out of the water."

"It's different now," I say. "There's medical evidence that you shouldn't go swimming for at least an hour after eating."

"Codswallop!" says Grandpa and he takes off his shirt.

He helps Grandma pull off her dress and then, taking her arm, guides her into the water. He's wearing the shorts he's had on all morning, and she's in her underclothes. At least they're not going to swim naked.

Melissa and I sit in the long grass above the stony beach. "They look like a couple of aliens," she says.

She's right. Grandma has a fat round body on skinny legs that have blue lines like tattoos under the skin. I think Grandpa was fat once upon a time, but now the fat has shrunk and the skin hasn't, so there are saggy rolls around his middle. They walk out very slowly, holding on to each other, and when the water gets deep enough, they dive under. I have to admit they are good swimmers.

"They're going out deep," said Melissa. "Doesn't look like they're scared of sharks."

There's no shade and we're sweating in our clothes, the sun, the gulls and the insect noises all mixing up somehow, like a hot chilli sauce poured over us. We finally agree that there are unlikely to be sharks in the shallows and we wade ankle deep, treading carefully on the stones and splashing water on our legs.

It's easy to see the old people because of the colour of Grandma's hair, but there is no sign of a triangular fin. Maybe there are no sharks at high tide.

They don't stay in long. I guess they ran out of breath because they come in puffing and walking even slower than when they went in.

They spread their towels on the grass beside us, and

sit down, and Grandpa puts his hand on Grandma's knee. "My Betty Grable!" he says.

Grandma gives a spluttering laugh.

He turns to us and winks. "Betty Grable was a film star in the 1940s. She had perfect legs, insured for a million dollars."

I look at Grandma's legs and look away again. Man, that is some sick joke!

She doesn't mind. She just gives him a shove and says, "Silly old fool."

10
MELISSA

It was extremely difficult talking to Mum and Dad and not being able to say anything much with *them* standing practically on top of us. But the phone has given me an idea. I dry the dishes for Grandma and ask, "Do you mind if I use your phone?"

"What for?"

"I – I – just a quick call to my friend Herewini. She's going to Queenstown soon and I – I want to say goodbye."

"Is it a toll call?" Grandma says.

I nod.

"When's she leaving?"

"Um, next Thursday."

"That's not soon, girlie." She limps over close to me, then says, "Tell me about your phone thingy."

"My mobile phone?"

"That's it."

"It has a battery, Grandma, that's flat, really dead. I brought a cord to recharge it but that needs electric power and you haven't –" I stop because my throat gets full and I might cry.

She puts her hand on my arm. "We might be able

to fix this. We get supplies from the mailman, Johnnie Proctor. Drives past twice a week. I write out a list for the grocers in Blenheim and he delivers it. Obliging fellow. I'm thinking he might take your phone home with him and recharge it."

My heart does a little flip. "Would he do that?"

"I told you, he's obliging."

"When's he coming?"

"Tomorrow. He'll be picking up a list from us, so you get me your phone thingy and its cord, and we'll put it in the mailbox with a little note."

I have to give her a hug. "Thank you, Grandma. You've no idea how you have saved my life."

"No idea at all," she says.

I help her to make out a list for the supermarket. With no fridge, they can't keep meat more than a day. There is a metal box with mesh sides, hanging under one of the macrocarpa trees. She calls it a meat-safe and she also puts butter and milk in it, anything she wants to keep cool. Yesterday, she bought a frozen chicken we're having tonight for dinner, but there'll be no meat after that, until an order comes in with the mailman.

On a spare piece of paper, I write a note for the mailman, asking for a phone recharge and saying please about a hundred times so he knows how important it is. I wrap the note, phone and charger, and put them in a bag ready for the mailbox.

With the phone sorted, the next thing I need to tackle is the bath. The bathroom in this bach is pretty well-named, because that's all it is, a room with a bath, extremely basic except, oh yes, there is a washbasin too, and a rail for towels. Well, anyway. I need to have a bath and before that can happen I have to clean four years of dust, dead insects and straw out of the bath. Don't ask me how the straw got in. I presume birds nested in the roof and bits dropped down through cracks in the ceiling. It looks really gross, so I ask Grandma where she keeps the vacuum cleaner, which gets a big laugh. I keep forgetting there's no power. I mean, I've always lived in normal houses. I have to use a brush and dustpan to get the trash out of the bath, no rubber gloves mind you, and then I need to give the tub a good scrub with detergent and hot water. At least now there is hot water. Grandma gives me hand cream but that does nothing for my Cinderella skin. The nails I've grown and shaped for the holidays will have to be cut back to school regulation bluntness.

While the bath is filling, I ask Grandma, "How do I wash my hair?"

"Eh?"

"My hair, Grandma. There's no shower, so how do I wash it?"

She says, "Didn't you see the saucepan by the bath?"

"I can't wash my hair in a saucepan!"

She snorts. "Girl, you use the saucepan to pour water over your head!"

Well, I tell you, that's how primitive this place is. I think I've already earned my thousand dollars.

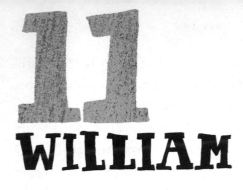

WILLIAM

I've calculated there's a circular driveway running around the garage and house, but the grass and weeds have grown so high you can't see it. It's a nuisance having to fight our way through waist-deep jungle every time we want to go to the garage or outhouse.

Grandpa says he must do something about it, and I imagine one of my jobs might involve mowing the area, but here lies a serious concern. There's no motor mower in the garage, the only grass-cutting devices being an old push mower, and worse, a scythe with a wooden handle and a pitted blade. I wouldn't have a clue how to use either.

On the way back from his swim, Grandpa pushes his way through the tall grass and brushes against some stinging nettle. He swears, and looks for some dock leaves to rub on his leg because apparently that's what you do when you don't have a chemist shop down the road.

"We have to say goodbye to this." He waves his hand over the wilderness of grassy weeds.

I wait for what he will say next, but he's busy rubbing green leaves on his leg, and when he's finished, he's thinking about something else. He says, "Can you drive a gear-shift car?"

"Grandpa, I'm not allowed to drive. I'm eleven!" I remind him.

"Well, what do you know? I thought you'd be at least nineteen. Ah, come on, boyo, I'm not talking about driving on the road. A gear-shift. You know anything about that?"

"Of course I know about cars, gear ratios, clutch, exhaust manifolds, pistons, I've read a mountain of stuff."

He looks at me, head on one side. "You're dead smart, aren't you?"

I shrug.

"Well, boyo, there's dead smart and there's living smart. You might like to put some of that car theory into doing. What say you?"

I look across at his old car, my mouth goes dry and I say nothing.

"If the car gets driven around, it'll flatten all this mess, a lot easier than cutting it, I reckon. You on for that? Don't worry. I'll be co-pilot first circuit or two, then you can go solo."

This doesn't make sense. How do you cut long grass with a car? Is he really asking me to do that? The sun makes me sweat and my skin itches. Me, actually drive?

That's what he means, all right. He opens the car, pulls the bench seat forward and then sits on the passenger side, his knees up around his chin. "Think you can reach the pedals?"

I climb in. Yes, I can reach okay, and I know which is which, clutch, brake, accelerator, clutch, brake, accelerator. I say it over, under my breath. It's hot in the car and there's a strong smell like oil and cooked plastic. I move forward on the seat and grip the steering wheel, which is almost too hot to touch.

"Great, kiddo. Now we turn on the ignition."

The engine starts and the car shakes with life like some racehorse at the starting gate, ready to bolt. I'm not scared, just naturally nervous. It would be fair to say that Grandpa is the last person on earth qualified to teach anyone to drive.

"Okay, okay, you see where first gear is? You put the clutch in and shift the stick up to first and then you slowly let the clutch out. Got it? In clutch, move stick, clutch slowly out."

I do that. I feel the clutch pedal go all the way to the floor and I hold my foot on it while I shift the gear stick with my left hand, making a slight directional error because I am right-handed.

"First, not third!" he says.

Now it's in first gear. I look to make sure, and take my foot off the clutch. The car leaps on all four tires and the engine dies.

"For crying down the sink, boy, you forgot to take off the handbrake!"

I don't want to do this. I open the door and jump out. "You forgot to tell me!" I yell at him. "You didn't mention the handbrake!"

He leans across. "Get in the car," he says. "Come on, get in! You'll be all right."

The nervous feeling is making me feel sick. I shout at him, "I hate this place!"

He doesn't shout back or even look mad, just nods and bites the edge of his thumbnail. "I guess this holiday is a bit of a dunger for you kids."

I squint at him. "Dunger?"

"You don't know what it means?"

"It's an old car. Like this."

He says, "Dunger's too good to be limited to cars. You can use it any way you like. You know what dung means?"

"Crap."

"You got it." He smiles squint-eyed. "Get in. We'll give this grass a thrashing."

I get back in. Dunger. Dunger, dunger, dunger! Most of my nervousness has leaked out and what I'm thinking now is, choice, I'm learning to drive his car, although I realise that's about as practical as learning how to shoe a horse since there are no cars like this where I live. Still, I am eleven, and I am going to drive. Just wait till I tell my mates.

I get back in.

The clutch is a bit jerky but the car goes forward, with Grandpa holding his side of the steering wheel because he knows where the driveway is. After two rounds there are clear tire-marks. That's when he tells me to put a foot on the clutch, and the other foot on the brake, so we can stop. He gets out. "Just keep the old girl in first gear, tama, and follow the tracks."

I'm so excited I can hear my heartbeat in my ears. Around and around I go, edging over slightly each time, watching the grass and weeds disappear under the bonnet. Most of the driveway is under the shade of the big trees but in two places I break out into sunlight and it's hard to see through the dust on the windscreen, then I'm back into shade again. After the fourth time, Grandpa steps out and holds his hand up. One foot on the clutch, one foot on the brake, put the gear stick in neutral, then yank on the handbrake. A perfect stop!

"Afternoon's getting on," he says, leaning through my window. "What say we speed it up a little? Second gear will be about right, to my thinking. When you've got it running in first, ease off the gas, put in the clutch, push the stick down to second, then give it gas as you take your foot off the clutch. Got all that?" I nod.

"Take off!" he says, waving his hand. He returns to the garage, without looking back. The first few times I try to change to second I forget the accelerator and the car stalls, but after that I get the hang of it and I drive until a wasteland of wild growth looks like a speedtrack, mostly flat dry grass with green patches of squashed thistles, weeds and nettles. I stop the car outside the garage and switch off the engine.

Grandpa comes out, wiping his hands on a rag. He looks over the circular driveway, flat as though a roller has been over it, and nods, but all he says is, "Did you remember to put on the handbrake?"

12
MELISSA

For someone who's nearly blind, Grandma notices things. After my bath, I come out to the kitchen with a towel around my hair, and she says, "You've cut your fingernails."

"I had to. They were chipped."

"What'd you say?"

I'm tired of shouting at her, so I don't answer. I don't know how I'm going to manage my wet hair without a dryer.

"Sensible girl," she says, pushing her hand inside the body of a chicken. It's lying in a roasting dish, a pale corpse with pimpled skin, and she's stuffing it with a crumb-herb mixture. "Can you play a guitar?"

"No." I unwind the towel. The heat from the wood stove is almost unbearable. It flows out of the kitchen, through the dining room and into the living area, which is already stewing in sunlight. "I had three years of piano."

"You've got the hands for guitar. My hands." She stretches her right hand, wet with chicken and breadcrumbs. Her knuckles are wrinkly and there are brown blotches on her skin, but she's right, we have the same width of palm, same length of fingers. I don't know if I like that or not.

"It's so hot in here," I say, shaking out my hair. "Can't we open a door or window?"

"Flies." She picks up the roasting dish and takes it to the stove.

"Your father had a guitar. Does he still play?" She doesn't wait for an answer. "He loved this place when he was young. He used to sleep in the same bunk you're in, liked stormy nights when he could hear the sea. What he didn't like was the trip out in the dark to the dunny. You know what he did?"

Of course I don't know. I watch the chicken go into the oven.

"He used to stand on the back doorstep and pee over the lavender bush. We wondered why it turned brown." She laughs as though this is some enormous joke. It doesn't occur to her that I might find it embarrassing. She shuts the oven door, puts more wood in the firebox, and says, "You're right. It is rather warm. Give me a hand to peel the vegetables, then we'll go down to the beach. Tide should be out far enough to get some mussels."

"What about the sharks?" I ask.

"Sharks? No big sharks out there."

"Grandma, you told me last night, watch out for the sharks."

"Did I? Heavens above, girl, you mustn't believe all

you hear, or you'll never survive on this planet. You'll find potatoes in that bag."

Potatoes, pumpkin, carrots. It doesn't take long and we escape from the heat of the kitchen. Grandma gives me a pair of old sneakers because my shoes would be ruined, she says, and I put them on although they look extremely hideous, with my toes showing through two frayed holes. But it's just as well I have them on – the tide is now so far out that the edge of the sea is just mud with small rocks sticking up. On these rocks are masses of mussels, green and black oval shells jammed together. I should tell you now that I don't like eating shellfish, but it is quite interesting gathering them.

I help Grandma down the beach. We have a knife and two buckets. The knife is to cut the beard on the mussel, which is the bit that holds it to the rocks. Grandma just pulls the mussels off with her hand but the shells are sharp, and my hands are still sore from scrubbing.

"Don't take the small mussels," she says. "And don't take the ones with a rough blunt end to their shells. They don't taste too good."

"Why?" I ask.

"Don't know," she yells back. "I never asked them."

The tide is still going out. Mud squelches under my feet and there are little yucky things like crabs and starfish and squishy sponges. I've seen them at Marine World but that's different from treading on them.

When we have half a bucket each, I take Grandma's

bucket so she can walk back with her stick. She is very slow, poking the flat stones in front of her before she steps on them, blinking, trying to see. She really is scared of falling. I tell her to stay where she is, and I run up to the road to put down the buckets. When I get back I have both hands free to take her elbow and arm and help her up the beach. Once she's on the road, she's all right.

She tells me to take the mussels to the tap by the garage and wash them. I do that. They have mud on them, and some little tube-worms.

So I get them as clean as possible and take them inside. "How are you going to kill them?" I ask.

"In a pot of water." She holds up a big saucepan.

"You're going to drown them in fresh water?"

She laughs. "I'm going to boil them."

I think I react, like with a shudder or something, because she laughs again. "You want me to give them an anaesthetic first?"

13

WILLIAM

Grandpa says his grandfather was only the second man in town to own a car, a Buick, he says, shiny black with big running boards and velvet seats, really posh, except he was accustomed to his horse and cart. So when Grandpa's grandfather drove to church with the family he forgot it was an automobile he was driving, and to stop it he called out "Whoa! Whoa!" and pulled on the steering wheel. The Buick stopped all right, halfway through the wall of the shop next to the church.

"Does Dad know that story?" I ask.

"Yep, he's heard it."

"Why hasn't he ever told it to us?"

"People remember what they need to remember," says Grandpa, rubbing his chin exactly the same way Dad does. "The rest slips through, which is just as well or our brains would self-destruct. Your dad was always quiet. Me and your grandma wanted a whole heap of kids but we just got this one boy, kind of gentle, always thinking. Don't know where he got that from."

I'm about to agree with him but I'm not sure how he'll take it, so I just nod. Besides, I wish he'd say more about the flattened grass that looks like newly cut hay. We are sitting in two metal folding chairs in front of the garage. The shadows are long and the air is full of dust and insects, bees flying home, sandflies and midges, big bluebottles that gather on the kitchen door because they can smell roast dinner. I say to him, "Dad did tell me about the wasps."

"Too early for them yet. They come late summer, and your dad was scared of them. He never got stung, but he was with me when one of those assassins got on my coffee cup. My lip swelled like a ripe marrow."

He pulls at his upper lip as though checking it is still there. "Bees sting once. Wasps go into a stabbing frenzy. Tell me, boyo, does your dad ever sing?"

I think he says "sting", and then I realise he's changed the subject. "Sometimes."

"He's always had a good voice. Used to march with us in the Vietnam War protests, serious little kid, seven or eight, singing at the top of his lungs, *We shall overcome…*"

"Dad was in a protest march?"

"A lot of us were. Good days. Nights of music, meeting in coffee bars by candlelight, playing guitars and drinking red wine. Your father would go to sleep with his head on the table, wrapped up in someone's coat. As for the marches, you wouldn't believe it, but people chucked stuff at us, tomatoes, eggs, sometimes worse. Called us communists." Grandpa laughs and slaps his leg. "Well, we did live in a commune."

This is something I do know. "In a geodesic dome made of metal and plastic."

"Metal and glass," he says. "Where'd you get the plastic idea?"

It was my father's description, but I say, "I don't know. Was it comfortable?"

"Nope. It was damned uncomfortable, but we were young then, and you know something, laddie? When you're young you put a romantic spin on everything."

"I don't," I tell him.

He puts his hand over mine. "Give yourself time. If you're lucky it'll happen. Right now, my stomach thinks my throat's cut. That chicken smells about ready. Wouldn't you say it was time for the F word?"

He keeps saying that and it's so tedious, but I smile and nod. I'm hungry too, and he's right about the chicken. The roasting smell is making the flies go crazy. I'm still waiting for him to comment on the flat grass. Although I did an exceptionally good job he doesn't seem to even notice.

There is no mention of it, but as we go up the back steps, he jerks his thumb over his shoulder and says, "If you can drive that car, you can drive anything."

We go in the house. I reckon you could cook a dinner on the table, the dining room is so hot, and without exaggeration, I feel as though I have to cut the air into chunks to breathe it. Grandma says, "We can't open any windows or doors because of these rotten flies, but they'll go when it gets dark and then we can air the house."

"Why don't you have fly screens?" I ask.

"We did," says Grandma. "Sea air rusts them after a couple of years. I've got more to spend money on than fly warfare."

At the mention of money I look at Melissa and wonder if we should say something about you-know-what, but the moment passes and Grandpa is offering to make the gravy.

There is something different about my sister. When I think about it, I realise her hair is hanging straight down her shoulders and she has no war paint on. "You had a bath?" I whisper.

"The water's hot," she whispers back.

"Everything's hot. I'd love a cold shower – if only there was a shower."

She leans closer. "There's something you should know, Will. I think Grandma was lying about the sharks."

14

MELISSA

You'll be interested to know that someone cleaned up the outhouse. I think it was Grandpa. Anyway, now it's not too bad if you avoid looking down the hole. The spider webs have gone, the wood has been scrubbed and there's a bottle of some dark fluid smelling like pine and tar that gets sprinkled when necessary. Since the outhouse is built on to the back of the garage, it's near the tap where I washed the mussels last night. There's a tin basin nearby with a bar of laundry soap, but no towel. I suppose we're expected to shake our hands dry. On that subject, I can't believe how sore my hands are, all red, with cuts from mussel shells. I show my hands to Grandma, but she can't see and thinks they're normal, which is probably also what she'd think if she could see them properly, anyway. I mean, it's this crazy pioneer lifestyle.

But back to the outhouse: in the middle of the night I had to go, but there was no way I was making that journey in the dark. A torch could supply a little circle of light. It's what's in the rest of the blackness, like wild pigs and possums and rats, you know, real scary stuff, that makes me break out in a cold sweat.

But I remembered the story Grandma told about Dad and the lavender bush, so that's what I did. Of course, there's no lavender bush now, just grass near the back doorstep. It's so close to the house that if there was a strange noise or anything I'd be back inside the door in a second. And no one will know, because there's a heavy dew each night.

This morning Grandma and Grandpa had another argument. I guess it's about spectacles or something when I hear their voices through the wall.

"You've forgotten, you silly old bird. Why didn't you put them in the case?"

"Aw, shut your mouth, there's a bus coming!"

By the time I'm dressed they've forgotten about it and he's helping her to set the table for breakfast. They're not lighting the fire yet, thank goodness — it's a cold meal of cornflakes and peaches. No toaster, no toast, so the follow-up is bread rolls and plum jam. Of course, Will is his usual greedy self. That kid eats enough for both of us.

My phone and charger are well wrapped and ready for the mailbox. Grandma says I don't have to do that yet, because the mailman won't be here till lunchtime, but I'm not taking chances. I slip on my sandals, the Italian ones with little silver bells on the thongs, and go out to the road. The sun is up but not too hot. There are gulls squawking over the water and bellbirds singing in the trees, sounds meeting each other like an orchestra tuning up. The day has a wet, fresh smell, even though it hasn't been raining, like all the air has just been scrubbed. After a while it hits me what the difference is: no traffic fumes.

The mailbox is a kind of long tin can on top of a post, and when I open the flap, I see it's full of birds' nests. More straw. Don't those stupid birds know they're supposed to live in trees? I rake the straw out, all of it, put in my phone package and Grandma's list, then close the flap and put up the red flag that will tell the mailman to stop.

Done. It's a good feeling, like being a prisoner and cutting through the first bars on the window. Well, actually I'll still be a prisoner, but at least I'll be able to text Jacquie and Herewini and some of the others, and find out what's happening in the world. My mind is so full that I don't look at my feet until I'm back at the house and I see that my designer sandals, worth two weeks of babysitting and shop work, are a wet mess, stuck with clay and grass seeds, and when I kick them off the dye from the red thongs has striped my feet. This place is so primitive that, honestly, I can't wear half the clothes I packed.

"That you, Melissa?" Grandma calls. "I found the guitars! They were in the back of the wardrobe, only we couldn't find the extra strings. They were in my guitar case, sure enough. Silly old fool couldn't see for looking. I need you to replace two broken strings for me."

I had this idea they'd have twelve-string country-and-western guitars but they're classical – one made of really nice, varnished wood, the other painted red with gold stars stuck here and there. It's the red one that has one string missing and another curled up like a cat's whisker.

"After that," says Grandma, "we'll go through that box of photos. I can't see the faces. If you describe them to me, I'll tell you what's what and you can write on the back of them." She points to a cardboard wine box filled with pictures. I don't mind too much. As a job, it beats scrubbing mouse poo out of cupboards.

I sit on the couch beside her. She's wearing the same clothes as yesterday and they smell of cooked food, mainly roast chicken. Her frizzy orange hair with its grey roots reminds me of a tiger. I don't know why, because with her sloppy mouth and hanging cheeks, her face is more like a hound dog. She's got nice eyes for someone so old, such a bright blue you wonder why they don't work well.

"How do you string a guitar?" I ask.

"I'll show you." She takes a length of nylon out of a packet. "Do you want to learn to play?"

I spread my chafed hands. "Grandma, I can't. My hands are too sore."

She snorts. "Nothing like guitar practice to toughen up your hands." She pokes the looped end of the nylon string at me. "You'll be good, girlie."

15

WILLIAM

I confess to a certain impatience to drive the car again, but that's not what Grandpa has in mind for today. One of the old macrocarpa trees has a split branch that is hanging down and resting on the ground, and he wants me to climb up and cut it off. The split is close to the trunk, and we have worked out that if I sit on the next branch I'll be able to reach over and cut it, although, just between you and me, I'm a little worried about the chainsaw. Certainly I'm not ignorant about chainsaws, but Grandpa's is heavy and old and I can't see any safety gear.

"How do I get it up the tree?" I shout.

"Get what up the tree?"

"The chainsaw."

He scratches in his ear like he's trying to hear better. "Who said anything about the chainsaw?"

Uh-oh. I look again at the branch, which is thicker than a power pole. Even though it's half broken, the wood is split in long interlocking fingers that will have to be cut. The other half is solid.

"Bush saw," says Grandpa. "It's light. You can carry it up on your shoulder." He fetches a saw from the back of the garage. It's shaped like a big D, with the blade – the straight part – wrapped in oily rags to keep it from rusting. After four years the rags have dried out, but the blade is still clean and the teeth feel sharp. He says to me, "Have you used one of these before?"

I shake my head.

"Easy," he says. "Use a light stroke. Push it too hard and it will bend. After a while it'll stick a bit, gum on the blade. I'll give you a kerosene rag to wipe the teeth when that happens."

I imagine that cutting a huge branch with this saw will be like painting a house with a toothbrush, but I'm happy to give it a go. Grandpa puts the saw over my shoulder, teeth facing backwards. There is a string tied to the saw. At the other end is an old paint can with a lid and handle, and inside, a rag swimming in kerosene. He says, "When you get up there, untie this here string from the saw and fasten it around the branch you're sitting on. When you need the kerosene rag, just pull the tin up."

It's an easy tree to climb, and by sitting on the good branch I can reach the one that has to be cut. The saw is another matter entirely, totally different from the crosscut and tenon saws we use in woodwork. For one thing, the teeth are literally the size of sharks' teeth, and for another, those teeth dig into wood like a row of chisels. As I wrench the saw free, Grandpa calls out, "Lightly, laddie! Don't force the saw or it'll bind. A light-as-a-feather touch lets it do the work."

He might be deaf, but he sees everything. He is definitely stronger than Grandma who needs help, especially with walking. Maybe that's because she's heavy – "Two pick handles across the backside," Grandpa says – or perhaps it's her inadequate sight. Whatever, I think I have better jobs than Lissy who has to be Grandma's eyes as well as hands in a house as hot as a steam bath. Through the branches I see smoke curling out of the chimney. That'll be for lunch.

Last time I climbed a tree was to get my friend Dave's kite, which was caught in a poplar. We have no real trees in our garden and sitting in this big old macrocarpa is very satisfying. It smells good, it feels good, and now that the saw is cutting I'm on my own, which also feels good. Grandpa has gone back to the garage.

Once you get used to a saw like this, it slides easily across the wood, the teeth eating the fibres and sawdust falling like snow. The wood is wet and has a strong tree-sweat smell – if I smelt like that, Mum would tell me to change my socks. I'm through most of the split stuff when the saw gets sticky. Time to rest my arm. Time to haul up the tin with the kerosene and wipe the blade.

From up here I can see a bit of the sea, a gannet diving head first, and the green bush at the end of the bay. The road is narrow and wrinkled with ruts; a private road, Grandpa says, owned by three families, so I guess that means you can do what you like on it. I wonder if he'll let me drive the car again.

The rag wipes the saw blade clean, and I manage not to cut myself on the sharp teeth. I lower the kerosene can and start cutting again, remembering, out of nowhere, a book about a man who put electrodes on plants to measure how much pain they felt. Why do I think of that at this moment? Sorry, tree, if it hurts.

My mates would like it here. Dave lives on a farm and he's got a kayak. The others, Seong, Anton, Buster, they're all into fishing. I'm sure Mum and Dad would enjoy a holiday in this place, too. I'll try to convince my mother that it just takes a couple of days to get used to it.

16
MELISSA

Grandma wants to show me some chords on the red guitar but I tell her my fingers are too sore, so we move on to the box of photographs. This will be a horrendous task, days probably, because I have to describe each picture to her, and then write what she tells me on the back. Some she doesn't recognise, and these, the easy ones, get dropped into a bag to be burned. Others have stories to them about people and places I don't know, although every now and then there's a photo of Dad as a baby with Grandpa and Grandma looking so young I hardly recognise them. Grandpa has a long droopy moustache and round-rimmed glasses. Grandma's frizzy hair sticks out sideways like a gorse bush and she has one of those peasant blouses that fall off the shoulders, not quite to cleavage level. She looks awesomely quaint. I hold a photo in front of her eyes and she says, "Is that my Indian wrap-around skirt?"

"Seems like it."

"Damn me if it wasn't just the niftiest thing. Indian cotton skirts and patchwork dresses. Leather sandals. It was all about being children of the earth."

"Dad says you made sandals from seaweed."

"Kelp. But it was a very brief fashion. They wore out in one morning." She laughs. "That photo was taken at a gypsy fair when Alistair was seven months old. Write it on the back."

There's a kind of slow, sick feeling bothering me, but it's a while before I realise what's causing it. Then it hits me with a thud. In sorting these photos she's preparing for the time when she's gone. She knows she's going to die. I'm now wondering if this entire holiday is a kind of goodbye to happy times in the past. The sadness of it blurs my eyes so I make a mistake and start putting good photos in the rubbish bag. She leans forward and yells, "You nincompoop! What are you doing?" and I feel embarrassed.

We have to stop to make lunch, which is homemade bread and mussel fritters. Neither Will nor I eats mussels, usually, but these have been ground up so they don't look like dead shellfish, and she's put in chilli and tomato and stuff, so they don't taste like it, either. We eat them with salad and they're actually amazingly good, and then, when I'm pouring everyone more lemonade, a car stops. The mailman! I run to the window. It starts up again, not a car but a red van, passing between the trees. Oh yeah, the man has picked up my phone!

I slap Will on the back. "He'll bring it back tomorrow!"

"No he won't," says Will. "Wednesday. It's twice a week, remember?"

No, I don't remember, but brother poo-face obviously

does. Well, Wednesday then. I come back to the table and continue filling the glasses. The kitchen is hot again and even the lemonade is warm.

Grandpa says, "You kids coming for a swim this afternoon?"

I look at Grandma. "You're absolutely sure there are no sharks?" I ask.

"Nobody said there were sharks," Grandma says.

"You did!" I tell her. "We talked about it and you told me not to believe everything I heard!"

"I never said there were sharks!" She glares at Grandpa. "He probably told you. Silly old fool, he'll say anything for a laugh."

"Be blowed if I did!" he said.

"Be blowed if you didn't," she replied.

He leaned over the table towards her. "Woman, you got a tongue in you so long, the back doesn't know what the front is up to."

I look at Will who shuts his mouth tight, glaring at me to remind me that I've started one of their useless arguments.

"You mean it's your ears," she huffs. "Half the time you don't hear what you're saying."

I have to interrupt. "Grandma, you told me there were sharks. Then when we went to get mussels, you told me not to believe it."

She turns to me, her eyes bright. "Never! I never said there were sharks. What I said was 'look out for sharks', which is entirely different."

At that, she and Grandpa laugh like mad, as though this is the comedy show of the year, and it's me they're laughing at. I am extremely disgusted with their behaviour. It's all a big act, a two-clown circus. It occurs to me that all their quarrels may be nothing more than performances for their own amusement. Well, I am not amused. But seeing as it's so hot, and considering there are no sharks, I will go for a swim after all.

17

WILLIAM

I'm learning about tides. High and low tide are about an hour later each day, and in this part of the Sounds there is a bigger than normal tidal difference, over two metres, which means if the outhouse was set in the mud at low tide, it would be covered when the tide was full. Today the tide is fully in at about 2.30pm but we go down earlier than that, while it is still crawling up the beach, since Grandpa and Grandma don't take much notice of rules such as no swimming after a meal.

Lissy is wearing a bikini about as big as three handkerchiefs, and the oldies have the same bathing gear they wore yesterday, their underclothes. We all have beach shoes. Grandpa is quite steady on his feet. It's Grandma who's all over the place, afraid of falling, so today we know what to do. Lissy gets on one side and I manage the other, so Grandma's held by the elbows and hands. We walk into the water together. It's not too cold and there are no waves, just ripples against knees, thighs, belly. When Grandma is up to her waist she shakes us off and dives in, reminding me of the big seal at Marine Park: clumsy on land, but smooth in water.

Grandpa follows her and they plough across the surface, out into the bay.

Lissy is fussing with her hair. "Will, let me have your swim goggles? Please."

"No." I'm fitting the goggles firmly in place. "You should have brought your own."

"That's not fair," she says. "I have to be Grandma's guide dog. You know I do. I can't get salt in my eyes."

"Then I suggest you shut them," I tell her, and I slide like a torpedo under the surface. Instead of heading out deep, I swim across the bay. The water is so clear, I can see rocks with clumps of mussels, shells slightly open, shoals of small fish that flash away in a shower of silver sparks, and red and green seaweed. There are no big fish. But I glimpse an arm in a screen of bubbles and see that Lissy is swimming near me. I come up and tread water. "Here! You can have my goggles. Don't lose them."

"Are you sure?" She stretches out her hand.

"If I wasn't sure, I wouldn't offer them. I'm going up now. You and Grandpa can help Grandma."

She grabs my swim goggles. "You haven't been in for very long."

"I've got something to do," I tell her, and I go back to the shore.

Now that I've cooled off, I want to finish the job on the tree before Grandpa gets back from his swim. I know he thinks I'm a city kid who knows fat zero about zilch, but I'm going to show him I can finish the branch. "I'll do the rest from the ladder," he had said, making a fuss about it being too dangerous for someone inexperienced. Inexperienced? Excuse me, please? Who was it spent more than an hour sawing at a branch that's about as thick as he is? I need to finish it. I have to make the last cuts and see that massive log crunch to the ground because, who knows, it might be as close as I ever get to felling an entire tree.

I don't stop for a towel or shirt, don't even change the wet shoes, but squelch back to the macrocarpa and the spread of sawdust that lies under the branch. I already cut three-quarters of the way through before lunch. Now the weight has caused it to split again, so that arrow-shaped fibres are sticking up. The bush saw is clean and sharp. I put it over my bare shoulder and climb back to the nearer branch. It will be easy to cut through the splintered wood, and after that, there isn't much left.

I have the knack of this now: light cuts, the saw slicing without resistance, dust falling, fibres parting. I imagine Grandpa's face when he sees the massive branch flat on the ground. He might get mad, but I'm ready with an answer about the difference between dead smart and living smart.

The tree creaks. More fibres spring up and then the saw gets caught in a cage of splintered wood. As I try to wrench it free, there is another creak that extends in volume to a loud crack. Fortunately, I let the saw go and swing my legs over to the other side of my branch. I don't know what makes me do that but it is just as well, because the cut branch gives way in unexpected fashion.

Instead of dropping, it rolls towards the place where my legs just were. There is another crack and it falls, tearing bark off the tree. *Whump!* It hits the ground. I'm shaken. I just sit there. What would have happened to my legs if I hadn't moved?

It's a while before I think about the saw. Where is it?

I climb down, look into the mess of wood and branches and see it underneath, Grandpa's bush saw bent like a paperclip.

I don't think I need to tell you what he says when he comes back from the beach. His face goes red, then purple. When he opens his mouth, he doesn't stop long enough for me to explain.

"You realise you could have bloody well killed yourself? Do you? Young jackanapes! You're as much use as tits on a bull. Didn't I tell you to leave it?" He stabs his finger at the air with each word.

Enough is enough. I yell at him, "*Vieux imbécile!*"

He is so angry he doesn't hear me, just goes on letting off steam like one of those whistling kettles. I walk back to the house, pretending I'm as deaf as he is.

I see him go into the bedroom and guess he and Grandma are changing after their swim. He's not mad now. He's laughing. His voice comes through the wall. "You know what? He called me a silly old fool, in French."

She laughs too, very loudly.

I've had enough of their craziness. I go back to the beach to talk to Lissy.

18
MELISSA

Day three. Seven days to go. Grandpa and Will have got over being mad with each other about the tree, but I haven't stopped feeling sorry for Will. He was only trying to do a good job. It's amazing that a little kid of eleven can cut down a branch nearly as big as a whole tree. "You did well, poo-face," I told him, and he said, "Thanks, slime-brain."

We should be used to odd things happening in this place, but day three starts with a different kind of strange. Yesterday, it was the bellbird chorus that woke us, this morning it's folk music somewhere outside the house, and at first I don't know who's making it.

You get to know people's voices by the way they talk. When they sing, it's a different sound. So it's a while before I work out that our grandparents are having a duet in the backyard. When I open the door I see them over by the stream. They're in their pyjamas, sitting in those funny old metal deck chairs, playing their guitars and singing a song about a Spanish captain who had a lady in every port. And you know something? It's awesome. They can really play, like proper musicians.

Grandpa flicks his fingers through the strings and rattles them on the wood. Grandma picks the melody. Their voices are a bit whispery but the song still carries right into the house. Will joins me in the doorway. It's very early, the sky is that grey colour before the sun hits it, and there are pillows of mist on the hill. Grandma's got a blanket around her shoulders. Her walking stick lies across her feet. She sings, "Put your shoes under the bed, the noble lady said, and we'll dance the night away."

I'm not sure if Grandma understands what that means, because if she did, I'm sure she wouldn't sing it, but her voice is amazing for an old lady. I glance at Will. His mouth is hanging open, like, is this crazy or is it crazy?

Grandpa sees us and raises his hand.

Will is in his shorts. I'm still wearing my sweetheart pyjamas with their pattern of flying pigs, and my hair is a mess. We push our feet into sandals and walk over while Grandma does some fancy flamenco chords to announce our arrival. Then they stop playing to talk to us. The bellbirds take over, chiming across the bay.

"We didn't mean to wake you up," says Grandma. "We came away from the house."

"Oh," says Will. "I thought you always played out here."

"Didn't want to disturb you kids," Grandpa says. "We couldn't sleep and the gee-tars were all tuned up ready to go-yo-ho."

A sandfly lands on my ankle and I slap it. "Sing something else. Please!"

Grandpa strums a chord. "Name it!"

"I don't know," I say. "Anything. Whatever."

Will says, "Sing something Dad liked when he was little."

So that's when they start "There was an Old Lady who Swallowed a Fly." Of course I recognise it because Dad used to sing it to me and Will, but I've never heard it with guitar accompaniment, lovely little arpeggios in the breathing pauses, string squeaks at the dramatic moments. The singing is good too, although the breaths come often, and Grandpa's chest makes a huffing sound. The music gets right inside me. I feel like I've just discovered a really interesting book that's been on the shelf all my life and I never knew it.

Grandma says to me, "You want to learn guitar?"

"Yes," I nod, and then add, "When my fingers are better."

"Me too," says Will.

We help Grandma back to the house. She's not wearing her glasses. I suspect she can't see a thing, and that all her playing is done from feel, which means she could play on a moonless night. Wouldn't it be something to perform like that? How much can you learn in seven days, I wonder?

Grandpa says he's so hungry he can eat an elephant, so Grandma gets out the cereal. "We'll have breakfast in our pyjamas," she says.

"I'd prefer mine in a bowl," says Will, trying to be smart.

While they are laughing at my brother, I set the plates and spoons on the table. "I think I'll buy a guitar."

"You might pick one up second-hand," says Grandma. "No point in getting something fancy until you know it's your thing."

I remember what she said about my hands being like hers, and I know, I just know I want to learn. "When do we get paid?" I ask.

Oh. I've said it. Will looks shocked. He sits up straight and turns to Grandpa. I put my hand to my mouth.

"You already have," says Grandma.

"What?" I remember manners. "I mean, I beg your pardon?"

Grandpa reaches for a bowl. "Your money went into the trusts last Friday, one thousand dollars each, and more when we can manage it."

"Trusts?" says Will.

"For your education." Grandpa looks at Will, then me, and he frowns. "You didn't think you'd get that amount of money to fritter away on rubbish, did you?"

We don't say anything.

Grandma sits down. "We've set up trusts for your future, one thousand dollars each. We'll add a bit here, a bit there. By the time you're ready for university it will have amounted to something."

I can't speak. My tongue won't work.

It's Will who says, "Do Mum and Dad know about this?"

"We talked it over with them," says Grandma. "I assumed they'd tell you the details. By the way, if you two want to learn the guitar, you can have mine. But that means you'll have to share it."

Will puts down his spoon. "Trust!" he mutters to me. "It's called a *trust*! What irony!"

19
WILLIAM

Plainly, our parents hadn't told us the details, because if they had, we wouldn't have come. So this news only adds to their degree of rotten, low-down guilt.

To say I'm annoyed is to call a hurricane a breeze. I mean there are degrees of anger, and when you have so much steam it wants to pop your eyes out, you have to do something about it. I can do nothing, nothing... except go outside with the axe and hack off the smaller branches from the big one I felled yesterday. I've never had an iPad – *bash* – or my own skateboard – *bash* – and now that will never happen – *bash* – *bash*.

"You watch your feet there, chico," Grandpa calls.

"My name is Will," I mutter, swinging the axe. *Crack!*

"You're chopping in the wrong place," he yells. "Aim at the underside of the branch, not the vee. It's easier."

Nothing in this place is easy, so I keep on chopping my way until he goes back inside.

I more than anticipated that iPad – I *visualised* it, worked with it in my head, bought apps for it, until it came into existence as already mine. Dad knew the money was going into a trust when he said "You'll be paid," and Mother-of-the-hundred-eyes, no, I mean *lies*, she knew about it too. No language has been invented to describe how I feel about their betrayal.

Melissa has come around to thinking the trust is a good idea, probably because she was going to spend her money on rags, anyway, and because she wants to go to a fashion design school which costs money. She wouldn't be Melissa if she wasn't thinking about herself.

My plans for the future are uncertain, but I may become a biologist or a meteorologist and go and work in Antarctica. Penguins and the weather are more predictable than my family.

"You can still get an iPad," Melissa says for the third time. "You just have to save for it."

"Stand back," I tell her. "I don't want to chop your toes off."

"Stop being a horrible little fart," she says, and goes back inside.

By mid-morning, that big branch has lost all its small branches, and its lower end is bare with sap bleeding out of a thousand axe cuts. There are still a few bigger branches at the thick end, but those will have to be cut by a saw and I fear the bush saw has outlived its usefulness.

I plan to take a walk by myself up the stream, so I can check on the water intake, but Grandpa comes out jiggling the car keys. "Want to come for a ride?"

My inclination is to choose a walk to the stream, but I look back at the car and become a swinging voter.

Well, not for long. It's the car that wins, because there is a chance, a real chance – but that doesn't mean I am happy about bending my principles.

"We're going to Hoffmeyer's farm," says Grandpa. "He's killed some meat. Has a leg of lamb for us. Not only but also, he's got a fifteen-foot runabout on a trailer and says we can borrow it for a day. Like to do some fishing?"

He gets in the driver's seat and gives me a couple of plastic bags to hold, but as soon as we turn out of the gateway and onto the road, he stops and gets out. "Move over," he says.

I move over in one quick bounce and grab the wheel.

"It's a private road," he says.

"I know."

He laughs. "No pedestrian crossings, no traffic lights, no cop cars. Just watch out for wild goats and pigs and an occasional landslide."

"Shall I put it in gear?"

"You've done first and second. Now you can try third. That's about top for this winding road. But you'll have to shove her back to second on some of the uphill bends. I'll show you when we come to that. Off you go, Stirling Moss."

"Moss? What does moss have to do with driving?"

"He was a racing driver before your time," says Grandpa.

I put my foot on the clutch that now feels very

familiar, and find first gear without looking. Clutch slowly out. The car rolls forward without a single jerk. I feed it more gas, then it's foot off the accelerator, clutch in, second gear, clutch out, accelerator, pick up a bit of speed …

"Now third," says Grandpa.

Easy-peasy, into third gear and we are cruising along the dirt road, which doesn't mean I am driving carelessly, far from it: there are ruts and potholes to be avoided and the occasional big stone that has dropped off a clay bank. I need to watch out for things like that. The road is narrow but there are curved clearings at the edge where I can pull over, in the unlikely event of another car appearing.

Driving is such a good feeling. I say to Grandpa, "Would you call this living smart?"

"I would, laddie, but don't tell your father."

I have no intention of saying anything to Dad. I have learned the sobering lesson that my parents can't be trusted.

20
MELISSA

Of course I'm disappointed, but it's not like the money has been taken away from us, it's been invested for the future, which is sort of old-fashioned and sweet of them. Rather like the photos, meaning they're thinking of a time when they can be with us in another way. I wish Will would understand this. He can't, and maybe I'm expecting too much from a little kid. Because he talks big, I forget he's only eleven. He is pretty upset, I can tell. He says this holiday is a "dunger", a word he picked up from Grandpa, and that he's never coming here again. But I noticed that when Grandpa mentioned the car, he changed his tune. Bet you anything he wants to drive.

It's photos again this morning, sorting them one by one. This picture is black and white: a man in tight swim-trunks with bulgy bits, on a diving board.

"Does he have glasses?" she asks.

"No. He's going to dive, Grandma! He's pretty cool, and he's got something around his neck."

"Shark tooth?"

"I don't know. Could be."

She takes the photo from me and holds it against

her glasses. "Stone the crows, girl, that's your grandfather. Put down the date – 1956."

Grandpa? That is so embarrassing! I recognise some of the other pictures. The little kid sitting on the beach with a dog is my dad, I can tell by his hair – Dad's hair I mean – and the big boy in school uniform is already the serious adult who wants to solve all our problems but usually makes them worse. I find pictures of Dad playing cricket, Dad on skis, Dad and his parents by a campfire, and one of Dad on a beach with a weird surfboard. It's just a wooden plank, round one end and curved in at the other.

"It's all we had in those days," Grandma says.

Most of the photos are of people that neither Grandma nor I recognise, which is just as well because we throw heaps out and soon the box is nearly empty, the job almost finished.

We stop, and I help her make a cold lunch. Not too difficult: lettuce salad, rice salad, hard-boiled eggs and watercress sandwiches. When I've set it out on the table, she says, "We're nearly out of bread. Do you want to make some new loaves?"

I think about it. "Yes, I would."

"Nothing much to it," she says. "If you do it now, it'll be risen after lunch when we light the fire."

It turns out that, like scone-making, there's nothing much to bread. What she calls a smidgen of salt goes into the flour. The yeast and sugar are stirred into warm water out of the tap, and for the third time she tells me I have her hands. Well, I have to say this, short fingernails are better than long ones when kneading bread, and I do like the touch of it. She tells me to put oil instead of flour on the bench to prevent it from sticking. Over and over it goes in a smooth white lump.

"Knead it until it feels like your thigh," she says.

Sounds odd, but that's the texture, although if my legs were as pale as this I wouldn't get into a bikini. I grease the bread pans and put two balls of dough in each.

She makes a clicking sound of approval. "Two big loaves. One for dinner tonight and breakfast tomorrow, and the other to take out fishing."

"Fishing?"

"It's not just the leg of lamb they're after." She jerks her head towards the road. "They're bringing back Hoffmeyer's boat. Your Grandpa's all set on us doing a day's fishing tomorrow."

I don't say anything. I can't go fishing tomorrow, I really, truly can't. At lunchtime the mailman will be bringing back my phone.

21
WILLIAM

When Mr Hoffmeyer shakes my hand, my knuckles crunch. He's a big guy, square shape, wiry hairs sticking out of the top of his black singlet, and more hairs on his legs bristling between the bottom of his shorts and the top of his gumboots. He looks like everybody's cartoon of a farmer. In his woolshed, he has a fridge without shelves, and inside it is the skinned body of a sheep hanging from a hook. He takes the carcase out, puts it on the bench, and with a meat chopper, *bang, bang, bang*, goes down the backbone, so the sheep falls in two halves. Just as quickly, he chops off a back leg and hands it to Grandpa who passes it to me. It's heavy, a lump of raw meat with streaks of white fat. I put it in a double layer of plastic bags.

I carry the meat to the car, wondering if all those sheep in the paddock know what I'm doing. Sheep are supposed to be dumb because they don't obey people's orders, but isn't that smart? Has anyone done research on the intelligence of sheep? For all I know, the animals staring at me as I walk over their grass could be making judgements about me as a carnivorous murderer, and telepathically planning their revenge. I put the bag on the floor between front and back seats and make a mental note to ask Dad if there have been any brain scans done on sheep.

Grandpa drives the car to the implement shed where Mr Hoffmeyer is waiting. Next to the tractor is a quad bike and next to that, a white boat on a trailer. Grandpa backs the car up close, then stops and gets out. So do I.

The runabout is a good size for four people, and has a 120 hp motor that Grandpa says is not fast, but adequate. While I'm looking at it, Grandpa lifts the trailer drawbar and swings it towards the car. But then he drops it. He steps back, leaning against the car and breathing hard. I run out to help, but Mr Hoffmeyer is already there, picking up the drawbar and dropping the end over the ball. He clicks it, and then does up the safety chain.

Grandpa is still huffing, holding his chest.

"You all right?" Mr Hoffmeyer says.

"Fit as a fiddle and ready to play." Grandpa straightens up and smiles, suddenly perky. He gets back in the car, the driver's seat, which is okay because I don't want to drive with a boat on this road, and I am left to say thank you to the farmer.

"You're a good boy," Mr Hoffmeyer says. "Look after your grandfather."

I want to tell him that I do, but also that Grandpa never says I'm good, never, and that I wish just once he'd see that I've been trying to do my best and it's not my fault if things go wrong. But that would sound a bit melodramatic, so I just shake hands again with Mr Hoffmeyer with a *crunch*, and get into the car.

Grandpa pulls up at the back of the bach, and Lissy brings Grandma out to look at the boat, although I'm not sure how much of it she can see.

Grandpa is breathing normally again. "We'll get the gear ready tonight, ready for an early start."

"Does it have to be tomorrow?" Lissy says. "The groceries are coming from the supermarket. Couldn't we go the day after?"

"Not a starter," says Grandpa. "Weather's packing up Thursday. Southerly bluster coming in, likely it'll last three days."

Of course, Melissa is not thinking about food being delivered by the mailman. With her, it's all about her stupid phone.

My sister has three brain cells, one for boys, one for clothes and one for texting messages to other girls with three brain cells.

22
MELISSA

Grandma wants to go fishing today. I seriously think she won't manage getting in and out of a boat, and I offer to stay home with her, but she is determined.

"I've always fished and I don't stop now. Only thing is, I can't see that damned nylon trace to thread the hooks. You'll have to do that for me."

Will's outside in the half-dark, helping Grandpa load the boat. Last night, they got the gear out of the garage, life jackets, rods, knives, cutting boards, two boxes full of hooks and stuff and some towels, and left it all on the verandah because of the overnight dew. Then, guess what, Grandpa and Grandma lit the kerosene lanterns and said they were going to teach us some chords on the guitars.

"The basic E minor chord first," says Grandma.

That is amazingly exciting. Will has the smaller red guitar because his fingers fit the frets. I have the big one that sounds dreamy mellow, like chocolate and cream. They show us three finger positions and then we actually play and sing Dad's song about the old lady who swallows a fly. It is really awesome. Afterwards, we both have crease lines across the tips of our left fingers, but Grandma says the skin will harden up soon enough. I think it already has. If we could stay home today I'd do more practice. I try that on Grandma, but she just says, "Plenty of time tonight."

Incidentally, the bread turned out to be excellent. I'm making meat sandwiches with it while Grandma fills bottles of water and lemon cordial for the picnic box.

The bellbirds are singing their hearts out. They have a long day, beginning before dawn and ending after dark, and it would be cool if you knew what they were saying. The chiming echoes from one side of the bay to the other and I think maybe someone could make a recording that is part orchestra and part bellbird sound. It shouldn't be too difficult.

What is going to be difficult is getting Grandma into the boat. I've been in a boat before and I know how this works. The boat goes in the water and we all climb over the side. But even with the three of us pushing, Grandma won't be able to do that.

I carry out the picnic box, the last thing to go on board. Well, I think it's last, but Grandpa sends me back for the low stool in the bathroom and a kitchen chair. I wonder why he wants to take furniture on a fishing trip, but he sets them up beside the boat. Well, how about that? Grandma is going on board before the boat gets launched.

Will gets into the boat to help her from that side. Grandpa and I are on each arm to guide her up onto the stool, then the chair, then over the edge into the boat.

With Will's help she settles in one of the seats and yells, "Ahoy, you landlubbers! Let's put to sea!"

Because I'm slightly sunburned from swimming, I'm wearing a hat borrowed from Grandma, the hideous T-shirt and the gross sneakers with holes and, oh yes, my very old jeans. Normally I wouldn't be seen dead in these but Grandpa says sunlight is stronger on water than on land, so it pays to cover up. On top of the shirt goes a more-than-hideous life jacket, and we're ready. Grandpa drives the car with the trailer-with-boat-with-Grandma-on-it out onto the road and then reverses down the access path to the beach.

He has chosen this time of the morning because the tide is right: almost fully out, the sea is at a place where the beach drops away steeply. He drives the car so that the back tyres are just in the water, then we all get out. Grandpa loosens the rope that holds the boat on the trailer. It slips back, back, with Grandma giving advice, until it's off the trailer and floating. Grandpa wades out to hold the boat. He turns it around so the back is facing us. "Okay, boyo. Take the car and trailer up the beach and park it by the road. Melissa, you climb on board."

"How? I'll get wet!"

Obviously, he can't hear me, and neither can Grandma. I yell louder. "I'll get my jeans wet!"

Will is already in the car, and the noise of the gear change sends a shiver down my spine. Bet they can't hear that, either. The empty trailer rattles as it bumps over the stones, and over the noise I hear Grandpa yell,

"You waiting for the next tide? Stop dreaming, girl!"

There's no way you can pull up the legs of skinny jeans. Even with the back of the boat pushed into the shallows, I am wet to the knees.

"Step onto the landing board and over the stern. Hurry up." That's Grandma's voice.

"All right, all right!" I yell back.

"Oh, my!" she says. "The princess got out on the wrong side of the bed this morning."

I climb into the boat. "The bottoms of my jeans are soaking!' I explain.

"That's the sea for you." She waves her hand. "But look at it this way, if it was the top of your jeans wet, you'd have some explaining to do."

I have to laugh. "Grandma, I can't believe you said that!"

She wags a finger at me. "Girlie, bear this in mind. I know what it's like to be thirteen but you don't know what it's like to be eighty-two."

"Fourteen, Grandma. I am fourteen and I'll soon be fifteen." I want to add that she lived in the age of the dinosaurs and my world is entirely different, but I can't be bothered putting all that into a yell.

"Whatever," she says. "A year or two makes little difference when you're my age. Now come over here. No, not that close, I don't want you dripping on me. Hand me the tackle box and I'll get you to make some nylon traces."

23
WILLIAM

I bet Melissa will tell Mum and Dad that I drove Grandpa's car. I hope she does. I want her to describe how I drove up the beach, towing a trailer, entirely on my own, over the stones and the grass of the access, then turned into a siding on the road and parked under a big gum tree. Handbrake on. Car locked. Grandpa couldn't have done it better. This will dispel the myth of the nerd who's not practical. When I was using the washing machine one day and it chose to flood, Mum told me, "Never mind, Will, you'll work with your brain and not your hands," which is a ridiculous statement, I mean, how does a brain connect to a computer without hands? I believe in all sincerity that a smart brain can teach hands to do anything. In a few days I have become a chopper of wood, a fixer of water, a student of guitar and the driver of a gear-shift Vauxhall. Which is why I'm surprised when Grandpa lets Melissa steer the boat.

"This isn't your job," I tell her. "You helped Grandma set up the lines."

"So?" She smiles. Her hair is blowing all over her face. I don't know how she can see to drive a boat.

I explain it to her. "You help Grandma. I help Grandpa. You cook. I drive. Understand?"

So what does she do next? She turns and yells at Grandpa, "Will says I shouldn't be driving the boat."

"He'll get his turn," Grandpa says, chopping up bait on a board.

Oh, all right, fair enough, considering she didn't want to come at all today and her sole training in boat skills has been making bread and scones. This is an echo of Mum's shop, where Melissa gets to serve customers while I carry heavy boxes of old magazines to the recycling bins.

I sit at the stern of the boat near Grandma, and put a safety pin swivel on the line on my rod, a simple task complicated by the way Melissa bounces the boat over waves.

We are now in the outer Sounds and the edges of hills have the sun on them, although the shadows are still dark. Our wake is astonishingly smooth compared with the sea on either side — I mean, you could ski behind the boat and feel you were on glass. The fringes of the wake are turbulent immediately behind us, diminishing to bands of white froth as far as I can see. Occasionally, a bit of seaweed or driftwood slides by, and something hard, wood, I expect, rattles along the bottom of the boat which I'm sure is called a keel, even on runabouts, and I think it's just as well for Melissa that it didn't smash into the propeller.

Grandma's voice is louder than the motor. She tells

me the names of the various bays and things about them, like the people who built their house around their caravan, and the man who ate everything raw, vegetables, fish and meat, because he said cooking took life out of food.

"See that hut? Doesn't look much, does it? An astronomer lived there. Came all the way from California with his telescope, to see Halley's Comet."

"Is he still there?"

She shakes her head. "I don't know and if I did know, I've forgotten. Over there is D'Urville Island. The bush was cleared by burning and when the smoke was over, the ground was littered with kiwi skeletons."

Too much information! There are some things you don't need to think about. But both my grandparents have an appetite for the sensational, a genetic trait that is lacking in my father and me, but occasionally apparent in my sister. Melissa has a flair for the dramatic.

At a suitable moment, I say to Grandma, "Did you know that Melissa stabbed an inflatable castle to death with her spiky shoes?"

Grandma laughs. "Yes, she told me. A pity no one filmed it."

That's exactly what I mean about being dramatic, my sister indulging in sensationalism even when she is responsible. The truth is she should have been too ashamed to mention it.

As we get close to D'Urville Island, Grandpa takes over the wheel and throttles back. He calls me up front to man the anchor. It turns out that anchoring a boat is not a simple matter. It requires knowledge of wind and tidal currents and the amount of chain and rope to be let out, approximately four times the length of the boat. This is a grapnel anchor like the skeleton of an umbrella, and suitable for these conditions, Grandpa says.

"How do you know it's suitable?" I ask.

"I just know," he says, which is not helpful to someone wanting information. Then he yells, "Right you are! Drop your lines."

Our bait is frozen pilchard, half-thawed and very effective. The second my sinker hits the bottom, there is a heavy tug and my rod jiggles.

"Wind it in!" yells Grandma. Her voice gets louder. "Oh boy, oh boy! I got one!"

We wind in two big cod, almost black, and swing them over onto the deck. They flap close to our feet.

"Get them off the hook," Grandma says. "Both of them. I can't see to do it."

I've caught fish before, herrings off the end of the wharf, and Mum or Dad has always taken them off the hook. It's not that I'm afraid of cod, simply that no one has explained the technique for doing this. I touch the fish's head and it goes into a spasm, jumping over my feet and tangling my line.

Grandma says, "Grab a cloth and hold it by its stomach. Go on, grab it! That's right. The spines can't hurt you. Now hold it firmly and work the hook out."

It is a very unpleasant task. I imagine how I'd feel

with a hook through my upper lip and then I think of the holes in Melissa's ears. She sticks earrings in and out and it doesn't seem to hurt. Her friend Jacquie even has a couple of holes in her nose – and I'm not talking about her nostrils.

Still holding the fish with the cloth, I drop it into the plastic bin. It thuds against the sides, desperate to get back to the sea. It's gross. I'm not super keen on fish and if I have to eat it, I'd prefer it came from a shop. But now I have to get the hook out of Grandma's cod. This one has swallowed the bait and the hook is deep inside. It all turns out a bit messy, and the fish looks quite dead when I've finished. I think of a lion biting a gazelle. I read somewhere that lions bite the back of the neck to break the spine so that their prey feels no pain. It would be good to know that fish, being cold-blooded, don't feel pain. That would be a logical assumption since they frequently take chunks out of each other.

Grandpa is taking Melissa's fish off the hook and that's okay because she hates wet and slimy things. We now have four cod, all in about five minutes of fishing.

Straight away Grandma gets another, but this time it's a small cod, pale brown. "Too little," she says. "Take it off the hook and throw it back."

I wrap the cloth around its belly and gently ease out the hook. As I throw the cod into the sea, there is a splash, a flash of silver and the little fish disappears.

"What was that?"

"What was what?" Grandma asks.

"A big fish, silver, maybe it's a shark."

"Barracuda!" she calls to Grandpa.

"Flaming barracudas!" he yells. "Lines up, everyone. No use fishing when the barracudas are around. We'll try somewhere else."

We all wind in our lines and put the rods in their holders.

"Hey, laddie!" Grandpa calls. "You pull up the anchor. Your sister can take the wheel."

Melissa takes off her hat, scoops her hair back and puts the hat back. "Don't worry, Grandpa. I can do the anchor. Let Will drive the boat for a while."

Cool! I go up to the skipper's seat.

She gives me a cheeky grin. "Your turn, snot-face," she says.

24

MELISSA

Grandma catches a snapper so big that Grandpa has to bring it into the boat with a net on a pole. "It's not snapper territory here, but she always does it." He taps his nose with his finger. "Don't know how. Magic maybe, she always was a cranky witch." He laughs and calls to Grandma. "You hear that? A cranky witch!"

"Envy won't get you anywhere, you silly old fool!" she yells back. "Are you going to fillet it? Or do you want me to do that too?"

"I might just chuck it back overboard," he says, "seeing it's too big for the pan."

She snorts. "That'd be more than your life is worth."

Grandpa lifts the snapper onto the board, and with a spoon, takes off the scales.

He cuts a huge fillet from each side, puts them in the salt water with the cod flesh, and throws the snapper head after them. "Lot of meat in that head," he says. "Best part of the fish." He stands up straight, putting his hand in the small of his back. "All done, snapper-witch!" he yells.

"I'll put a spell on you!" she yells back.

"Woman, you did that years ago. If you hadn't, I'd have walked right past you."

I wish they wouldn't do this. Will says it's all an act, but I see fight in their faces. They're like hissing cats, fur prickling with electricity, then laughter, then sparks again. They don't care who's listening. And please don't think I'm being goody-goody. I understand that it's perfectly natural for a couple to argue when they are getting to know each other, although when I find the right partner, I am sure that won't happen. He and I will discuss things while holding hands, which is some extremely good advice I read in a magazine. You can't fight while holding hands, it said. Our differences will never become rows.

I never knew Mum's father, but her mother, my Granny Margaret, is very calm and gentle and romantic in her own quiet way. Every time she changes the sheets on her bed, she also changes her husband's bed, although he's been dead nearly sixteen years. That is so sweet. I think I will be like her.

Grandma is having a go at Grandpa. She's out of her seat, calling him names. He comes back to stow away the tackle box and when he passes her, he reaches around and pinches her on – oh, that's so gross!

Fortunately, I need to pull the anchor up again. The chain and rope get stowed under the hatch, and by then Grandma and Grandpa have had to stop yelling at each other because the motor is going and they can't hear.

It's midday and we pass around the meat sandwiches.

Will is steering us towards the Sounds and I can't help but think of the mail delivery. It has taken us two hours to get out here, so I suppose it will be the same going back to the bay.

What I don't estimate is the time it takes to get the boat back on the trailer when we arrive. All I want to do is jump over the side and race up to the mailbox. Instead, I have to stand in the water with Will and hold the boat while Grandpa goes off to get the car. When the trailer is backed in, the three of us have to wind in the rope. "It's not an automatic winch," Grandpa tells us. "Just use elbow grease." Which is his way of saying hard work. I'm sure it would be much easier without Grandma's weight on board.

When the boat is secure on the trailer, we hop in the car and Grandpa drives up the beach to the road. There is a cardboard carton sitting beside the post, and the flap of the mailbox is slightly open. My phone is there! It's in the same wrapping I put around it, but the plastic and paper is loose and, yes, it is fully charged! Fabulous! I know I should help Will and Grandpa but I've waited so long for this. I switch it to connections and press Jacquie's number. The sign comes up. No service. That means no reception at the mailbox. I'll need to go up to the house. I stand on the verandah and press again. No service. In the living room. By the garage. No service. I don't believe this!

I have to go up the hill. There'll be reception on high ground. I run past Will and Grandpa who are helping Grandma out of the boat, and I splash across the stream and go up the hill to the edge of the bush. No service.

When I arrive back at the house, Grandma is sitting on the couch with her feet up. She says, "Have you caught up on all the gossip?"

I can't answer.

"You're a bit young to be going deaf," she shouts.

The tears come. I can't help it. "There's no – no cell phone reception in this stupid place!"

"No what?"

I yell at her, "No reception! This is the end of the earth! People don't live like this any more!"

She swings her feet off the footstool and stands up, holding on to the arm of the couch. Then she lurches towards me. I put my face against her shoulder and cry and cry. She pats me on the back. "Light the fire," she says. "After dinner you can use our phone."

25
WILLIAM

I tell Lissy she should never gamble because she has so much bad luck. She calls me a turd because she thinks I'm being mean, but I honestly feel sorry for her. All this fuss about recharging the phone, and then she finds out there's no reception. Grandma, the Duchess of Tightpockets, amazingly offers her free toll calls to Queenstown, but none of Lissy's friends are answering. The best she can manage is Mrs McKenzie whose twins had gone on a day trip to some cattle station. With luck as bad as that, I wouldn't even buy a raffle ticket if I were her.

I take back everything I said about a mild dislike of fish. The fried snapper is brilliant, especially now it looks like food and not some dead creature. Before dinner, I hosed down the boat while Grandpa put the gear away, and now we're ready to take it back to the Hoffmeyers.

"They won't be there," Grandpa says. "They were going to the North Island this afternoon. But we'll take a bag of cod fillets and put it in their freezer."

As we walk to the car, Grandpa looks up at the sky. It has misted over with a greyish-yellow look and the air is very still, a sure sign, he says, of an approaching storm. "It'll be here in the morning," he tells me.

He drives us to the Hoffmeyers' place, and backs the boat and trailer into the implement shed, at which point I remember him holding his chest when he tried to hitch the trailer to the car. So I jump out. "Let me try, Grandpa!"

"Too heavy for you, kiddo," he says. "But you can help."

He puts down the jockey wheel on the trailer, then undoes the chain and clamps. We get on each side. One, two, three, heave! We try again. One, two, three. I dig my feet in and pull with all my strength. Hee-ee-eave! The trailer comes off the car and we step back. Grandpa is puffing. He gives me the plastic bag of fish and waves me towards the house. "Freezer," he says. "Kitchen."

I look at the house, dark and quiet. Even the dog kennels are empty. "How do I get in?"

Grandpa is leaning against the wall of the shed. "Key under mat."

It feels a bit like breaking and entering, except that the key is under the doormat, which is next to a pair of gumboots, and the door opens as though it has been expecting a visitor. Over the fence, about a hundred sheep stare at me as I go inside. In the laundry, actually before the kitchen, is a chest freezer. I open the lid, put the fish in and head back out, locking the door and replacing the key. The sheep are still staring. When I run back to the implement shed, they break into a run and stream away, rattling across the paddocks. Maybe they are not intelligent after all.

Grandpa sits in the passenger seat with his knees close to his chin. He's still huffing. Lifting the trailer has knocked all the wind out of him and it's a while before he can talk easily. He shows me how to switch on the car's headlights. We have another two hours to sunset, but the sky is pressing down and making darkness. "Off you go," he says. "Drive carefully."

The road is familiar, so is the car, and the space between Grandpa and me is comfortable. He says, "Wasn't that snapper something to write home about?"

"It was good." I hesitate for a moment, then ask, "Why do you and Grandma fight?"

"Fight?" He sounds surprised.

"Yes. Argue. Call each other names."

He shifts in the seat and I think he's laughing but I'm not sure. "You're too young to know." Then he says, "Why do you think we fight?"

I keep my gaze firmly on the road. "If you really want to know, I'd say you two are incompatible."

"Incompatible?" He snorts. "You mean I've got the income and she's pattable?"

"Grandpa, you know what I mean. You and Grandma don't get on together. You torture each other."

He laughs out loud and I feel my face get hot. It's that old pecking order again, adults rejecting truth from kids. When he stops laughing, he says, "You are totally lacking in judgement, boyo."

"That's an oxymoron," I tell him.

"Really? You know some big words."

I don't dare take my eyes off the road. "If something is total it can't be lacking."

He laughs again. "I'll oxy you, you little moron. Just drive us home."

26
MELISSA

It is exactly 1.25am on the fifth day, and I have to go to the outhouse. This can't be a quick trip to the grass by the back door, and I don't know what to do. I've tried going back to sleep because Dad said intestines slow down when we're sleeping, but this is getting extremely urgent, and I simply cannot go out to that hellish black hole in the dark.

I try to think of other things, like last night, the grandparents off to bed early and Will and me practising the guitars by lantern light, eating his milkshake lollies, and getting to feel the frets without looking. It sounded good. I showed Will how to pick, easy as long as you are holding down the chord, and keeping to the rhythm, strong first beat: pluck, da, *da*, da, pluck, da, *da*, da. It felt good. But under the good feeling was a tension that wouldn't let go, and I knew what it was about: my phone charged up and useless. Isolation! What's the use of a smart phone in an unsmart place? We might as well be in confinement in some eighteenth-century penal colony. I'm sure it's the phone business that's disturbed my stomach.

I really have to go. I switch on Grandma's torch and tiptoe into the living room. Will is sprawled over the couch, tangled in a sheet as though he's been fighting with it. I shake his shoulder.

His eyes fly open. "Who's that?"

"Me. Will, I need you to –"

"What's wrong?" He sits up quickly.

"Nothing's wrong. I have to go to the loo, and I can't go on my own. Will?"

He groans and lies down again.

"Please, Will. I'm desperate. You need to stand guard in case something comes."

"Like what?"

"Wild pigs, rats, creepy things. Oh, please, Will! This is very urgent!"

Grumbling, he gets off the couch and picks up his torch. He leads the way out the back door, across the grass and past the garage, to the outhouse. There is no moon, no stars. Everything outside the torch beam is black, and the air is cool, very still, as though it is waiting for something to happen.

"Why do they have the outhouse so far away?" I ask.

"Flies," says Will. "Bad smells."

"Oh." I wait while he opens the door. "Can you go in and check it?"

"What for?" he says.

"You know, spiders, rats. There might be something down the hole."

He goes in, waves his torch around and comes out. "All clear."

"Wait outside. Please, Will! Don't go away."

"Well, hurry!" he says.

I go in, shut the door and shine the torch down the hole, double check, before I sit. "Are you still there, Will?"

"Yeah, yeah!"

This is so primitive! Jacquie is staying at a motel. Herewini's aunt has an awesome townhouse overlooking the lake. No one, absolutely no one in my entire school, will be pooing over a hole in the earth in the middle of the night.

A cold draught comes up, as though answering my thoughts, and I shudder. "Don't go away, Will!" I call.

"I'm still here." Then he says, "Tough biscuit about your phone."

What? It's so unexpected that at first I'm suspicious. But no sarcasm follows and I think he might be sincere. "Thanks, Will."

Through the gap at the top of the door, I see moving torchlight, which means he's testing the darkness. He says, "Those two fight a lot, don't they?"

"Yeah."

"They don't care who listens to them. When I was driving back tonight, I told Grandpa they were incompatible."

"You said what?"

"You know – incompatible."

"Oh Will, you didn't! What did he say?"

"He just laughed like I was talking nonsense. Lissy, do you get the impression they think they're normal and we're not?"

"What made you tell him that!" I am embarrassed for my little brother. "Do you know what incompatible means?"

He makes a coughing noise.

"Will?"

The coughing, hissing sound gets louder and is followed by a squeak. "Lissy!"

"Stop that noise!" I yell at him. "Stop at once! Will?"

"It's not me!" he yells back.

I finish in a hurry, scared by the panic in his voice. "Wait for me!" I call. "Don't go away!"

The only answer is another round of coughing and hissing, like we're being attacked or something!

"Will, are you there?"

There's a great crash on the roof, close to my head.

I'm out that door so fast! I run like mad towards the house.

When I get to the back door, I shine the torch towards the outhouse and see something moving on the roof. It looks like a cat.

"It's a possum," says Will who is in the kitchen, shivering.

"All that noise from one little possum?" I start to laugh.

Will laughs too. Actually, it isn't all that funny but we laugh and laugh until our sides are aching and we're gasping for breath, and then, because the kettle on the stove is still hot, we make ourselves some cocoa and open a packet of Will's biscuits.

27
WILLIAM

The rain starts before dawn, at first lightly brushing the roof, then getting so loud that it drums out conversation. The temperature has dropped too, so nobody minds when Lissy lights the fire for breakfast. There is plenty of dry firewood stacked on the verandah. I bring wood inside and put it on the hearth while Lissy cooks crumbed fish and fried eggs with tomatoes.

We tell Grandma and Grandpa about the possum but I'm not sure they hear us. They are tired after yesterday's fishing trip and they walk as though dragging heavy weights. After breakfast, Grandpa goes back to bed for extra sleep, and Grandma brings out her battery radio from the bedroom, tuned to some talk programme. No music, just blah, blah about threatened fish species. We all had fish for breakfast. But saving the planet is always about what other people should be doing, never us. Right? I tell Grandma that and she says, "Shut your cake-hole, boy, I'm listening to the wireless."

Lissy needs more firewood, so I go out to the verandah to get an armful. I can see the bay through the trees, grey, choppy and blurred by heavy rain. The wind is coming up and swirling rain in over the verandah. No bird-calls this morning, only water noises, rain on the iron roof, rain on the road and underneath that, the roar of a rain-filled stream.

Inside, we hear rain hissing in the chimney, but the fire is bright orange and the oven is hot.

"Want to make some bread?" Lissy asks.

"Not particularly."

"Go on," she says. "It's easy."

For once she's right. It is easy, and with Grandpa asleep there is nothing else to do, although I resent the way Lissy makes me scrub my hands twice over before I start, as though I've been handling cyanide. Kneading bread reminds me of playing with modelling clay at kindergarten, and the way we'd flick it off our rulers to make it stick on the ceiling. I have no doubt that bread dough would work just as well, but fortunately I have outgrown the desire to try it.

While the dough is rising, Lissy and I have a game of Scrabble. I win, as usual, and she says I cheated, as usual. I tell her I don't know why anyone with such a limited vocabulary would want to play Scrabble. She gets so annoyed that she takes over the bread-making and won't allow me to put the loaves in the oven. I appeal to Grandma. I mean, what kind of logic confuses a word game with baking bread? But I think Grandma is on Melissa's side because of the useless cell phone. She not only allows my sister to finish the bread, she also tells her she can use the bach phone to contact her friend Herewini in Queenstown.

Melissa goes to the phone. The process is easy enough, turn the handle three times and when someone at the telephone exchange answers, you give the number you want. But that is too difficult for my sister. "No one is answering," she says, "There's a strange crackling noise."

"It's the possum ringing its friend," I tell her, but she doesn't laugh so I say, "Here, I'll do it for you."

I grind the handle, lift the phone and wait. Actually, she's right. There is no voice, merely a crackling sound. "Something's wrong," I shout at Grandma.

"Storm," says Grandma. "It'll be a tree over the line somewhere. Don't worry. They'll be in tomorrow to fix it."

I ask, "How will they know to come in and fix it, if we can't tell them it's broken?"

"Don't ask silly questions!" Grandma says.

I think it is a perfectly reasonable question and it's her answer that's silly, but I will not waste time in argument. I look at Melissa, who is close to tears, and I don't tell her that this is just another example of her persistent bad luck.

28

MELISSA

Will is one of those kids who get bored easily, like a grasshopper on hot sand, Dad once said, although it's just Will's head that tends to be hyperactive, thoughts bouncing from one thing to another with no gaps in-between. What is extremely annoying is his need to always be right. He'll create arguments out of nothing, just so he can have the last word. It is very tiring.

I remember the day he started school. He was really cute then, this cool little kid who wouldn't let go of my hand. My friends thought he was adorable. Now they see him as a gigantic pain. I sincerely hope he grows out of it.

The bread comes out of the oven, two perfect loaves. Does that please him? No, he wants to know why the oven doesn't have a thermometer on the door, and the answer – that it is a very old stove – does not stop him.

"Why not put a thermometer on it? It would save guesswork and failure."

Grandma doesn't answer. I think her deafness is sometimes selective.

He stands in front of her. "I'm surprised you and Grandpa haven't thought of doing that."

"Oh, shut up, Will," I tell him.

So he turns on me. "I kneaded your bread dough for twenty minutes, all my work put into an oven of unknown temperature. Is that practical? It could have burned. It could have been raw."

"The bread is perfectly cooked."

"That's sheer chance!"

"No!" I tell him. "Grandma told me when to take it out. She could smell it."

He will not give in. "The oven door needs a thermometer. They could easily get one and stick it on with heatproof glue and then you'd know —"

He doesn't finish the sentence, because Grandpa appears, rubbing his hands together. "A good afternoon for the garage!" he says to Will.

Grasshopper Will is onto the next thing. "What are we doing?"

"You know those surf-casting rods in the roof?" says Grandpa. "We can take the reels to bits and fix them. Have you ever cast from the beach for snapper?"

"I've read about it," Will says.

"That's like reading about swimming," Grandpa says. "But I'll show you and your sister. You can have a rod each."

Will gives me a look, like the glare when Grandpa asked me to drive the boat, but he doesn't say anything. I smile at Grandpa and say thank you several times.

Lunch is potato and watercress soup with warm bread, then Grandpa and Will go out to the garage, taking one of the lanterns because the day is so dark with rain.

Grandma switches off her radio and gets out her knitting: big needles, thick wool. She has a large plastic bag full of knitting yarns, and I sort them into balls of different thicknesses. While I'm winding a skein of green bouclé wool, she says, "I'm told you don't like our conversations."

I look at her. "What conversations?"

"Your grandfather and I. You and your brother have a problem with the way we communicate." She puts her knitting down in her lap, which is her way of expecting a response.

I'm nervous. She's been told whatever it was that my stupid brother said to Grandpa last night. "You mean – Will?"

She doesn't answer, just stares at me with those strong blue eyes that are about as useful as my phone.

I go on winding the green wool. "It's just – just that you seem to fight a lot."

She nods. "Is that what you call it? Fighting?"

"Um, well, yes, it sort of sounds like it."

She grunts, then says, "We're not around kids much, these days. It's easy to forget how young you are." She picks up her knitting and pushes one of the thick needles into a stitch. "So you think we fight, eh? I'll tell you this, girlie. You have to be very close to have that kind of freedom, very close indeed." Two more stitches and she says, "What about you and William?"

I look at her.

"You fight," she says.

"That's different," I say. "He's my brother. He's not —"

"Not what?"

Since she's asking, I have to say it. "I just know I will *never* fight like that when I have a husband!"

She laughs. I've told her something seriously serious, and she's treating it as a joke. I remember Will suggesting that she and Grandpa thought they were normal and we weren't, but that doesn't stop me from feeling angry. I sort out an appropriate answer. "I believe there's a peaceful resolution to every problem," I tell her.

There is another burst of laughter, and she says, "I said the same things at your age!"

I put down the ball of wool and make the excuse that I need to go to the outhouse. The rain is heavy and there is no such thing as an umbrella, but there is a sheet of plastic by the door that I can put over my head. I run across the sodden grass and fling open the wooden slat door. How dare she say that I am like her! Imagine it! Comparing my little brother and me to an old married couple! I know she's old and probably getting dementia, but really, there is no excuse. I sit for ages, thinking about it. She always has to have the last say. That must be where Will gets his overwhelming desire to be right from.

Water thuds on the outhouse roof, reminding me of last night's possum. With the plastic sheet over my head, I open the door.

As I go towards the house, Will comes running out of the garage. He almost bumps into me, stops, stares at me like I'm some kind of monster. His face is wet. He looks terrified. "Grandpa!" he whispers.

"What's wrong?" I ask.

He starts to cry. "I think Grandpa's dead."

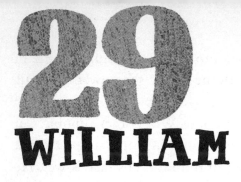

29

WILLIAM

It happens like this. We are going to take the reels off the surf-casting rods that lie on a rack under the garage roof. The rack is like a little mezzanine floor under the peak, too high for us to reach, although I can see the ends of the rods sticking out like handles on a wheelbarrow.

Grandpa looks around. "Where's that ladder?"

We both remember where it is, against the macrocarpa tree I cut the day before yesterday, only now the rain is pouring down like a waterfall and neither of us wants to go out to carry a wet ladder. We look through the curtain of water that falls over the door. Grandpa says, "Likely as not our water pipe'll be washed out again."

"I'll go up the stream tomorrow and fix it," I tell him.

"Tomorrow's no good. You have to wait until the flood subsides." He pats me on the head. "Nature's a good teacher, laddie. When there's tons of water outside, you've got to be careful with it inside. Pipe gets washed out, no water running into the tank, you can't fix it until the stream's gone down. Good excuse for not having a bath."

"What about the ladder?" I ask.

He's not listening. "Look at those trees in the rain. You ever notice the way they produce branches the same design?"

I say yes, but I don't know what he's talking about.

"No matter what tree you look at, the branch is the same shape as the tree it's growing on. Look at the pine, the manuka! Every tree! That's nature for you, boyo, design expert number one. "

"The ladder!" I remind him.

"Forget the ladder," he says, turning back into the garage. "This'll do it." He tips a round drum of oil on its edge, and rolls it under the surf-casting rods. "Give me a bit of a help up, eh?"

We should do it the other way around. I don't weigh too much. If Grandpa lifts me high enough, I can reach the rods, but for some reason, I don't tell him that. Instead, I let him put his hand on my shoulder so he can hoist himself up on the drum. He stands, feet together inside the rim, and raises his right arm. His hand is shaking. He brings it to the end of one of the rods and holds on for a moment, as though he is thinking what he should do next.

"Can I help?" I ask.

He doesn't answer. His hand comes down and rests at the top of his jacket as he makes that huffing noise. It was what he did at the Hoffmeyers' place, a sound somewhere between a fast breath and a cough.

"Grandpa?"

Then he falls sideways. It happens too fast for me to do anything. He just drops. Like the tree branch. The oil drum skids across the floor with a screech and Grandpa's head hits the floor.

"Grandpa, are you all right?"

Of course he isn't all right. His eyes are almost closed and his face is the same colour as the concrete. Blood comes out of his nose. I try to lift his head up but it falls back again. I pull my hands away and there is blood on my fingers.

That's when I run out into the rain and see Lissy.

"Grandpa!" My voice is choked.

"What's wrong?" she says.

30
MELISSA

He's lying on the floor in a dark pool of blood, his right arm bent up behind him. I kneel and place my fingers on his neck. He's not dead. There is fluttering movement under the wrinkled skin. "Can you hear me?" I shout in his ear.

He doesn't move. I get a tissue from my shirt pocket and wipe the blood running from his nose. "He's alive. Unconscious. Go and get Grandma."

Will runs to the house while I sit on the garage floor. I don't know where his head is bleeding, but I fold up the sheet of plastic and put it under, so he's not lying in the blood. When I move him, his eyelids flicker. "Grandpa?" But there is no other response. His face is grey and there are dots of sweat on his forehead. "Grandpa, are you awake?"

We have to get help. There's an emergency helicopter that flies into remote places, but could it come in this weather? Then I remember, the phone's not working, so how would we contact them? I have an idea. Will can drive. He can go to the neighbour's place, the people who lent us their boat. Will knows where the key is. He can use their phone, maybe get an ambulance. How long would it take on this road?

Grandma stumbles across the grass, stick in one hand. Will supports her on the other side. They have no coats and are very wet. Their hair sticks to their scalps and Grandma's glasses are spotted with rain. As she comes into the garage, she tries to run. She would have fallen too, but Will and I grab her just in time, so she just sort of sinks down beside Grandpa. "You silly old fool!" she yells at him. "What have you done, you useless beggar?"

"We'll phone for an ambulance," I tell her.

"Something's wrong with his arm," she says. "Why is it bent like that?"

"We'll go to the neighbour's phone."

"Help me lift him." She grabs his shoulder. "Roll him over so we can free his arm. Come on!"

We half lift, half roll him, and pull the arm out from underneath. It is covered by the sleeve of his woolly jacket, but even so, it looks a funny shape. Grandma sits on the floor with Grandpa's head and shoulders against her skirt. She is feeling along his scalp. "It's just a flesh wound. He's concussed. I think his arm's well and truly broken. We have to get him to hospital."

Maybe Grandpa hears the word hospital, because he groans and I see some of the worry go out of Will's face. It's a groan of pain, but it means Grandpa is alive and waking up.

I say to Grandma, "Will can drive the car to those

neighbours – you know, where we got the boat. He knows where the key is. He can go in the house and phone for the ambulance. They won't mind. It's an emergency."

"No good." Grandma shakes her head. "If our phone is out, theirs will be out too. We're both on the same line."

Grandpa groans again.

"Standing on a drum at his age!" says Grandma. "You'd think he'd know better. We'll just have to take him to hospital in the car."

Will stands up straight.

"Who's going to drive?" But as I say it, I realise it's a silly question.

"William, do you know how reverse works?" she asks.

He shakes his head.

"Now's the time to learn," says Grandma. "Back it up to the garage. Melissa, you go into the house and get my purse and the tartan rug out of our bedroom. Hurry!"

"Grandma, you're soaking wet," I tell her. "You need to get changed."

Grandpa opens his eyes. He looks at us and gives another groan. "What a dunger!" he says.

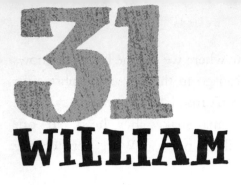

WILLIAM

Melissa insists that Grandma and I change into dry clothes, but even then, no one is ready. They keep going back for stuff, a sheet ripped in half to make a sling for his crooked arm, some cushions, paracetamol for pain plus a bottle of water, a spade in the back in case we have to dig our way out of a rock fall, towels, a bag with his medication and pyjamas because he might have to stay in hospital. But while all this is going on, two good things happen: Grandpa wakes up enough to get in the car, and the rain slackens to a drizzle.

Backing the car was slightly horrendous because I nearly ran over Grandma who was behind me giving orders. I thought it was Melissa who was directing me, and I could see her. I didn't know there were two of them.

"I'm not exactly invisible!" Grandma yelled.

But she was, because I couldn't see in the rear vision mirror. So Lissy suggested I sit on one of the cushions, and that is much better. Driving the car in reverse gear is no big deal as long as I keep a light touch on the accelerator.

While we're waiting, I watch Grandpa in the back seat.

He doesn't say much because he still hurts – a bandage around his head, his arm in a sling, dried blood on his neck, a blanket over his knees, like he's a victim of some hit-and-run accident. It's his eyes that have come right, fully focussed, two marbles rolling together, ping, ping, noticing that I don't have the handbrake on. He says slowly, "If a tyre rolls over your sister's foot, she won't be able to wear her castle stabbers."

I laugh and put on the handbrake. His memory is okay.

Grandma gets in the back seat with him, and Lissy's in the front to help me see the road. She also helps by putting on the windscreen wipers and the lights so any oncoming traffic can see us through the rain. I confess to feeling nervous about meeting a large truck on a narrow part of the road.

"We'll deal with that problem when we come to it," says Lissy, and although that advice is entirely useless, it is more acceptable than our grandmother's ongoing comments about the idiot who stood on an oil drum. I suspect that anger is her way of downloading shock, but it gets a bit stressful, especially when I'm trying to focus on the road.

The distance to Hoffmeyer's farm is familiar. I know the bends, the trees that line the road, and I remember what Grandpa said about branches looking like miniatures of the whole tree. I can't believe that was only two hours ago.

"How fast am I going?" I ask Lissy.

"Can't you see?"

"I don't want to take my eyes off the road."

She leans towards the dashboard. "Forty kilometres an hour."

We splash through clay-coloured puddles and Grandpa groans. "Mind the bumps."

"Sorry. How far is it to Blenheim?"

Grandma answers for him, "Two and a half hours. You're doing well, Will."

I'm not so sure. It's all right on this road with no traffic, but what happens when we get to the main highway? What about traffic cops?

"Damned fine thing I taught him to drive," Grandpa says. "Remember when I taught you to drive, my little gooseberry tart?"

"You taught me a lot of things," says Grandma. "Half of which I was too young to know."

They laugh and I hear Lissy snort and mutter, "Too much information!" I want to remind her it's their deafness that makes personal conversation public, but I am too busy watching the road through the rain, which has thickened. I peer over the top of the steering wheel and ask her, "Can you make the wipers go faster?"

The cloud is so low, it rests on the tree-tops. On some outer bends on the road, wind gusts drive rain against the car with a sudden rattle as though it is hail. The sea is choppy but no longer all grey. Near the shore it is a yellow-brown colour where clay from the land has been washed into it.

When we go up a hill, I forget to change into second gear, and the car stalls with a jerk. No one says anything. As I lift my foot off the brake, we begin to roll backwards. Quickly, Lissy pulls on the handbrake. I turn the key, the engine starts, and I push the gear lever into first. We are facing uphill. "Go on," says Lissy, still holding the handbrake. I shift my foot over to the accelerator and slowly let out the clutch. As the wheels roll forward, Lissy releases the handbrake and slides it down. We go up the rest of the hill in first gear and when we get to the top, I change into second and then third.

"Thanks," I say to Lissy. Then I ask, "How did you know to do that?"

"I watched you," she said.

32
MELISSA

The water has loosened clay on some of the banks, so there are slips and little heaps of yellow dirt on the road. Luckily, nothing so serious that we have to stop and get the spade out of the back of the car. Will just drives around them. But on the other side of the Sound we come to a tree lying across the road. It's a skinny little manuka, but it's still attached to its upturned roots in a mound of mud nearly as big as the car. There is no way we can move it.

Will and I stand in the rain, staring at it. We have a blunt spade to shift dirt but no saw or axe to take care of a tree. We tug at the manuka, which is no thicker than my wrist, hoping that it will break, but it keeps whipping back to its original position. It's about half a metre above the ground and it blocks the entire road.

"This is ridiculous," says Will.

I agree. "We need your bush saw."

"It's not my saw, and anyway it's busted. There's a rope in the car. Maybe we can tie it to the top of the tree and pull it up high enough for the car to get through."

I shake my head. "That's too hard. Let's try the other way, push it against the ground and drive over it."

We lean on the skinny manuka tree and it sinks a little. Then we both sit on it. It feels like a spring beneath us. We could bounce on it all day and not break it.

"We don't have to push it right to the ground," Will says. "If it's just above the road, the wheels will do the rest."

Grandma has wound down her window. She puts her head out. "What's happening?"

Will and I look at each other, thinking the same thing. "Will she do it?" Will asks.

I walk back to the car and brush my dripping hair away from my eyes. "There's a little tree across the road. If we push it down, Will can drive over it."

"Then push it down," she says.

"I've tried sitting on it, but I'm too light."

She doesn't even grumble. She grabs the door handle and swings her feet out to the muddy road. Will and I help her over to the tree and find the right place for her to sit. I sit beside her. It works. The springy tree collapses under her weight and settles close to the road.

Will runs back to the car. There isn't much space between Grandma and the edge of the bank, but he drives carefully, edging the car into the gap. As the front wheels touch the tree, it moves as he said it would, down against the ground, then *bump*, *bump*, the car is over it and on the other side.

I help Grandma to stand. We are both wet but she is not complaining. "Where there's a will there's a way," she says to Will when he comes back with a couple of towels. He grins, and neither of us tells her that people quote that one at him all the time. Usually, it comes from teachers who want him to do better at sport, but from Grandma it's a compliment.

We sit in the car to dry ourselves. We're on a hill overlooking the arm of the Sound, water everywhere on land running down into the sea. Through the rain we can hear the rush of waterfalls, even though we can't see them. Grandpa is quiet now. I think he's in a lot of pain. His head is on a cushion against the window; his eyes are closed but he's not asleep.

We have only half an hour before we reach the main road that will take us to Blenheim. Will is worried about taking the car into traffic. I'm sure he can do it all right, but people will see a little kid at the wheel. I wish I knew how to drive. At least I look about the right age.

My hair is no longer dripping. I feel in my bag for my hairbrush, and my hand stops on my phone. Something makes me pull it out and switch it on. "Hey! I've got a signal!"

Will is drying his head. "You're not ringing your friends!"

I hold up the phone. "It's a strong signal. Three bars. Grandma, you hear that? My mobile phone is working!"

"That's a no-brainer!" says Will. "Put the stupid thing away!"

"Shut it, poo-face! We can call the hospital!"

Grandma leans over my seat. "Can you ring that thingy from here?"

"What's the hospital number?" I ask her.

"You don't need that," she says. "Just call 111."

33
WILLIAM

Another problem solved. I don't have to drive on the main road to Blenheim. An ambulance is going to meet us at Havelock, at the beginning of the road. Grandma arranged it with the hospital. She shouted so loud she hardly needed Lissy's phone.

"Why do we meet outside the public toilets?" I ask.

"Because I need a restroom, stupid boy," she says. She leans close to Grandpa who doesn't open his eyes. "Oil drum!" she snorts. Then she yells at me. "Don't just sit there! Get moving!"

No one talks for a while. I think we're all hoping that Grandpa will wake up and make one of his stupid jokes, but that doesn't happen. The only sounds are car noises: the swish of the tyres in the wet, and the soft thump of the windscreen wipers. We're now on a sealed road, still lots of bends, but no more mud and bumps. Lissy has fiddled with the ventilation controls so warm air is coming in. We need that. Wet clothes are cold clothes, even in summer.

Lissy says, "There's a red truck behind us. I think he wants to get past."

I can't see in the rear vision mirror. "Is he close?"

"Very."

"There's no place to pull over," I tell her.

A horn sounds behind us and I jump. It's a loud aggressive sound, two blasts meaning "get out of my way".

"Idiot!" yells Grandma.

"Can you drive faster?" Lissy asks.

Panic always makes me feel sick. "No. No, I can't drive faster. Look at the road! One bend after another."

"He's right behind you," she says.

The driver blasts his horn again. That does it. There's nowhere to pull over so I stop on the road. The truck stops behind us. Now I can see it, bright red and just one person. It's not a man. It's a woman and I think maybe she'll get out and come over to our car. She doesn't. She backs a little, and then drives past us.

Grandma has wound down her window. "Take a long walk over a short jetty!" she yells.

I don't think the woman hears her. She just looks at me, her eyes opening up like she's seen a ghost. I want to shout, "I can't help it if I'm small," but she is past us. Her truck spurts exhaust fumes and is out of sight in seconds.

"Do you think she'll report me?" I ask.

"Nah," says Lissy. "She's too full of herself."

I put the car into gear. I admit to being exceptionally pleased that I don't have to drive further than Havelock.

The road gets wider and straighter, the cars behind me can pass without difficulty, and because there's so much rain and mist, I don't think anyone notices me sitting behind the wheel. Although it's not yet six o'clock, the sky is heavy and all the cars have their lights on. The weather may make driving difficult but it is definitely in my favour, although that doesn't stop me from thinking every white car we see might belong to a traffic cop.

The white vehicle we want to see is already in Havelock, an ambulance, sleek with rain, parked right outside the public restrooms. It's so conspicuous that even Grandma spots it from a distance. "It beat us!" she says. "Well, how about that!"

There is no parking space behind it, so I pull into the kerb in front, and switch off the engine. Grandma has her window down, head out and is yelling. "Hey! Over here! This is what you're looking for!" Nothing happens so she says to me, "Sound the horn, Will."

I press my hand on the middle of the steering wheel. It's a loud noise, a bit like the red truck that followed us, and it gets attention. The driver's door of the ambulance opens and a guy gets out, official uniform and stripes on his jacket. He walks quickly to Grandma's window, glances around the car and sees me at the wheel. He has round eyes and a small black moustache. He points a finger. "You? You, the driver?"

"We didn't have too many choices!" Grandma yells.

A woman in the same uniform is approaching. "Amanda!" the man calls. "You're not going to believe this!"

34

MELISSA

While the paramedics put Grandpa on the stretcher, I help Grandma into the restrooms. She doesn't want to leave him. She keeps looking back, but she has to go to the toilet. When she comes out of the cubicle, she has her skirt tucked up. I pull it down for her and help her to wash her hands. They are shaking so much, the soap stuff drops onto the bench. "Silly old fool," she says to herself, and I realise she is really frightened.

When we come out, Grandpa is in the ambulance, a blanket tucked around his legs, and both the man and the woman are bent over him. Will is still in the car. Some people have stopped on the footpath, to see what's going on. I want to tell them to mind their own business. This is my grandfather, not theirs.

Grandma says to the paramedics, "I guess one of you will have to drive our car to the hospital."

The woman turns, shaking her head. "No. You all come with us. The car will have to stay where it is. Just take any valuables and lock it."

Grandma doesn't argue. Will is told to sit up front with the driver. Grandma and I go in the back with the woman. Grandpa lies opposite us and now has a needle in his arm with a tube connected to a plastic bag. There is a mask thing over his nose and mouth.

The woman says he has been given medication for pain and is sleeping. But I don't think he's asleep. He looks limp and grey, the way he did when he was lying on the garage floor. To tell the truth, he looks extremely unconscious.

The woman keeps checking his pulse. She reminds us that her name is Amanda.

I tell her everything I know about Grandpa's fall, the cut on his head, the blood, his twisted arm.

"Did he just lose his balance or did he faint?" she asks.

"I don't know. My brother saw it happen."

"Why do you ask?" Grandma wants to know.

"Has he been having fainting spells?" Amanda asks.

"Nope. Never." Grandma says. "It was that damned fool oil drum."

Soon after that, the ambulance goes faster with the siren on and Amanda smiles at us. "That's for the young man's benefit. We're very impressed that a nine-year-old could drive all the way —"

"He's eleven," I tell her. "Eleven and a half. He's just small for his age."

"Well, anyway, I think our driver is just showing him what we can do," Amanda says, glancing at Grandpa.

I know she is lying.

The ambulance goes directly to the back of the hospital and Grandpa is put on a trolley, with the plastic bag hooked on a pole. Will and I stand back, but Grandma is holding onto the trolley and firing questions at him. "You okay, darl? You're in hospital. Remember the ambulance? Hey, tiger! Can you hear me?"

Grandpa's eyelids flicker and open. He pulls down the mask and says to Grandma, "Here's mud in your eye, kid," and then he shuts down again.

Everyone who talks to us is cheerful and efficient, but no one tells us anything useful. Grandpa is wheeled away and we are put in a waiting room that is warm and quite comfortable, except that we are extremely uncomfortable with worry. Grandma complains about the chairs that are too soft and too low to get out of, and how she won't sit in those high-backed rubbish chairs, also, the magazines are useless because she can't read, and no, she doesn't want instant coffee that tastes like pee, thank you very much.

We don't say anything. What's the point?

A nurse comes in with a clipboard. Well, we think she's a nurse but she turns out to be a doctor. She asks the same kind of questions that Amanda asked in the ambulance, wanting to know if Grandpa had fainting fits.

"Never fainted in his life!" Grandma says.

Will says, "I thought he was going to faint two times."

The doctor looks up. "Why did you think that?"

"He was huffing," Will says.

"Anything else?"

"When he huffs he goes a funny colour," says Will. "Like now."

"Interesting," says the doctor.

"Interesting?" barks Grandma. "What the hell do you mean by interesting? Where is he?"

"He's fine. He's with the cardiologist now but you'll be able to see him in a few minutes."

Grandma looks as though she's going to explode. "Cardiologist? For a broken arm?"

The woman pats her on the arm. "I'll be right back," she says.

That's another lie. I take out my phone, and this time Will doesn't say a word. He knows I'm calling Mum and Dad.

35
WILLIAM

I think I've been asleep. I know this is the hospital waiting room, but it looks different, shifted somehow, like turning over too many pages in a book and getting to a different part of the story. There's a cushion under my head, a grey blanket trailing on the floor. Lissy is standing near me, and Mum and Dad are talking on the other side of the room. Mum and Dad! Where has Grandma gone? I look at the clock. That can't be right. 4.20am?

"You're awake," Lissy says.

"Unnecessary statement," I mumble.

"You had a good sleep," she says. "You were tired."

I'm about to repeat the unnecessary statement line, when I realise she's not being sarcastic. "Where's Grandma?"

"Ah, Will!" Dad gets out of his chair, strides across and pats me on the shoulder. "Congratulations are in order. That was a fine effort!"

"It was an effort for a *fine*," Mum says, standing up. "I hope no one reports you for underage driving. You should never have been put in that situation."

Lissy laughs. "We'd just have to tell them it was our parents who put us in that situation."

I push the blanket aside. "Where did Grandma go?"

"She's asleep in a bed next to Grandpa," says Lissy. "She was exhausted. The doctor said her blood pressure's very high, not good at all."

I look at the clock again. I've been asleep for more than seven hours, my last memory being of Lissy on the phone to Mum at 9.00pm. Seven hours and twenty minutes out of my life!

Mum and Dad are standing together, and almost, but not quite, holding hands. I anticipate announcements, and am not far wrong.

Mum begins. "We're all shattered. We've booked a room at a motel. We can catch up on sleep before I drive you back to Christchurch. First thing, though, we'll go to Havelock to pick up Grandpa's car. Dad will keep the car in Blenheim until they're ready to go home."

Dad says, "Mother will probably be out today. Dad will be in a little longer. He has a double fracture of the right arm, both radius and ulna. At his age that probably means surgery with steel plates and screws. He won't be driving for a while. But that's not the main concern. It's his heart. They're going to insert a pacemaker and he'll be right as rain." He stops, reading something in our faces. "It's not a huge operation," he says. "A wire is threaded into the heart. The pacemaker itself sits in a pocket of skin in his chest. It will make a big difference."

Lissy says, "What about the rest of the holiday at the bach?"

"I'll be taking the two of them back to Timaru," says Dad.

"But the bach isn't locked!" I tell him. "The garage was left open."

He smiles. "I don't think there's anything there that a burglar would want."

"Don't worry," says Mum. "We'll fix that later. We've got some good news for you. Mrs McKenzie phoned. She said you'd called her when the twins were out and this is what she's offered. If we put you on a bus to Queenstown, you can stay with them for the rest of the holidays. Both of you! Isn't that wonderful?"

I look at Lissy. We don't say anything.

"You can pack tomorrow," Mum says.

"Our clothes are still at the bach," Lissy says.

Dad shrugs and holds out his hands. "Look guys, we're doing our best. This is a very complicated situation. We'll get the old folk back to Timaru and then we'll think of sorting out the bach and your clothes. Right?"

"You've got heaps of clothing at home," Mum says.

I look at Lissy again and she says it for me. "But what if Grandma and Grandpa don't want to go back to Timaru? What if they want to stay on at the bach?"

"Impossible," says Dad. "Entirely out of the question."

"They could go back to the bach if we went with them," I add.

Dad laughs and says, "Who would drive?"

"You would," says Lissy.

36
MELISSA

All that seems a long time ago, although it's less than three weeks. Yesterday Dad drove Grandpa into Blenheim to get some stitches removed. Today being hot as an oven, all Grandpa is wearing is his old khaki shorts and the plaster cast on his arm. He is showing off the scar on his chest.

"You're looking at a real bionic man!" he says to Grandma, his hand over his pacemaker. "You want to feel my electronics?"

"They should have done your brain while they were at it," she says.

"No, I've got you for that," he says. "Brain hot-wired to your mouth." He turns to us. "You know something, kids? She even argues with herself."

Outside, the chainsaw splutters and roars. Dad has fixed it and is using it to cut up Will's macrocarpa branch.

Will gives a backward nod towards Grandma and Grandpa. "Truce didn't last. They're fighting again."

I shrug. "Oh, I don't know. I think people have to be very close to each other to have that kind of freedom."

"What?" He looks as though he is tasting something bad. "Melissa, that's a screwed-up philosophy!" and then he goes out to help Dad with the wood.

He is such a child!

Today I am doing the washing, and am very pleased that Mum is not here to see Grandma's method of cleaning clothes. You throw everything in the bath, fill the bath with hot water and soap powder, then get in and tread on the clothes. That's it. You just keep on walking up and down, then let the soapy water out and run fresh water for rinsing. After the rinsing water goes down the plughole, you squeeze the clothes with more stamping. But get this! The next thing is to bring in the wheelbarrow, yes, the old garden wheelbarrow, right into the bathroom, and put a sheet of plastic in it. On top of the plastic you throw the wet washing, then you wheel it outside to the clothesline. Now, I know you're not going to believe this, but it's actually extremely easy, what Grandma calls beach laundry.

Mum would have a fit.

Our mother has explained to Mrs McKenzie that we're very grateful for the kind holiday offer, but we have to look after our grandparents. It was difficult to leave so many things unfinished – just one chord on the guitars, fishing rods not fixed, much more swimming to do, and learning to make different kinds of bread – and now, especially now, impossible to leave with the Hoffmeyers' seventeen-year-old son Conrad home from his summer shearing job, tanned skin, crinkly hair and a smile like melting golden syrup. Also, I've nearly mastered the art of snorkelling and clearing my mask. I mean, there's so much to do here!

Mum says she might come up next weekend. Then again, she might not. I tell her I'll put a vase of flowers in the outhouse just for her, but she just grunts and says she's busy at the shop.

Dad has taken three weeks' leave and he's having a ball, running around the bach, finding things he's forgotten, telling us about the scrapes he used to get into, like the time he and some friends made a raft and borrowed a man's outboard motor. It fell off into the sea and they put it back on the man's boat without saying anything. It was useless, Dad said, all seized up with salt. I'll bet Grandma and Grandpa didn't know that.

At home, Dad sometimes sings in the shower. Here, he sings a lot, all day. We all do. We have concerts at night with the guitars and Will and I are learning a whole lot of folk songs like "Shenandoah" and "Lonesome Traveller." There are also songs that would make Mum's hair curl, like the one about the sailing ship. *The first mate's name was Carter, and gad, was he a farter. When the wind wouldn't blow and the ship wouldn't go, they got Carter the farter to start her.* Will just loves singing that. And the graveyard song. *The worms crawl in, the worms crawl out. They go in thin and they come out stout. Oo-oo! Oo-oo! Ah-ah! Ah-ah! How happy we will be!*

I'm the one that's had three years of piano practice and Grandma says I have guitar hands, but you know, it is Will who is extremely fanatical about learning, and he's good, I mean he knows more chords than I do, and he's begging Grandpa to teach him flamenco, that Spanish music that sounds like planes taking off. My brother's such a strange child. The other day Dad mentioned the money in the trust for our education and he told Will maybe he could save up for an iPad. Will simply stared at him. I swear he'd entirely forgotten about the iPad and all that betrayal business he talked about.

I'm going to make ravioli next weekend. I don't think Mum will come, but Grandma will show me how to make it, little pasta purses full of ricotta cheese and herbs, and maybe we can invite Mr and Mrs Hoffmeyer and Conrad for dinner.

Oh, I forgot to mention that Will always sleeps in the top bunk now, which is good in case a mouse comes in at night. I usually go to bed late, but tonight he is still awake when I come into the room. He says, "Do you think Grandpa is going to die?"

"Everyone dies," I say.

"You always give such pathetic answers!" His voice sounds muffled and I wonder if he's been crying.

"Grandpa is going to live for ages. Didn't you hear him say he can walk up stairs now without getting breathless? The only problem is his arm and that will soon be better."

"I thought he was going to die." The same muffled voice.

"Will, Dad says those two are as tough as old boots."

He is quiet for a moment, then he says, "Lissy, do you want to go to Queenstown next year?"

"Why do you ask?"

"I'd rather come back here," he says.

Actually, so would I, but I'd find it extremely difficult to explain that to my friends who think Queenstown is heaven with frills. "We'll talk about it in the morning," I say. "Good night, poo-face."

"Good night, slime-brain," he says.

For a while I listen to his breathing, then I say, "You know, I'm sure we could talk Mum into coming, too."

But the only sound is from the wind outside. Will is already asleep.

THE END